THE PILGRIMS

MUHAMMAD ASIF NAWAZ

LIBERTY Publishing

Published by Liberty Publishing

C-16, Sector 31-A, Mehran Town Extension,

Korangi Industrial Area, Karachi, Pakistan

1 2 3 4 5 6 7 8 9 10

ISBN 978-627-7626-280

Acknowledgements

O grief! Now you tell me,
For this puzzle remains unsolved.
Whether a restless heart is concealed within me,
Or am I a restless heart?

- Shaad Azeemabadi

Dedicated to all the restless hearts who informed mine, to all my fellow pilgrims whose trajectory through this journey shaped mine.

My father, for giving me the strength to experience all that I have, and my mother for being the ideal aide throughout this convoluted maze. Without you, there's nothing.

My sisters, Uraida, Zaeema, Aiza, Yasra, Fatima, for being my strongest supports and for keeping me grounded - by not reading my book or giving scathing reviews, for example.

My wife, Mahreen, also the first reader of the book, who was as important a part of this book as she is of my life. Thank you for bearing with me as I re-thought and re-wrote this book, and for forcing me to stop with the edits.

My daughter, Jehan, who has absolutely nothing to do with my book, but everything to do with everything in my life.

To my friends who religiously read all the bits I texted them at all times of the day, and told me this book was worth being out in the world. Samreen Agha, Huzaifa Azim Butt and Haroon Ashraf - your valuable critique shaped this book into what it is. Tashfeen Abbasi, Haseeb Sultan, Rutaba Tanvir, Muhammad Orakzai, Yasir Saood, Syed Zain, Anhum Malik, Nihal Farid and Umair Sarfaraz - had it not been for the green signal you gave, this ride would have faltered. If you do not like this book, it is on these people.

To the team at The News. Lubna Khalid and Fatima Zakir. Had it not been for the former, I wouldn't be writing today. Had it not been for the latter, I wouldn't have attempted a novel.

To the people who have read me before, and told me, at times dubiously, to quit my day job and pursue writing.

To all the people who helped me navigate through the murky waters of publishing. I'm grateful for the grace with which they took me on. Raza Rumi, Osama Siddique, Mehr Hussain, Sauleha Kamal, and very importantly - Awais Khan. Kindness begets kindness - I'm forever indebted to all of you.

To the cities that became characters in this book, Lahore, Sukkur and Islamabad. And to the swathes of Dera Ghazi Khan, where I started writing this book as much out of inspiration as boredom.

To the rich traditions, culture and history of the land I belong to. If nothing else, I'd want this book to be remembered as a tribute to these.

To Aariz, Bina, Mehar and Feroze - the characters of this book. They shared their lives with me for one sweet stretch, engaging me completely, and then relieving me of the burden of sharing their stories and going their own ways.

And to you, holding this book in your hand currently. Words have a way of finding their own audience. And since The Pilgrims has landed in yours, I am sure it was meant to come to you.

Prologue

THE GREAT Sufi saint Lal Shahbaz Qalandar was once wandering through a desert with his friend, embarking on a pilgrimage. As is typical in the deserts, the temperature was searing during the day, but became exceedingly cold as the night fell. They knew they needed fire to warm themselves up; otherwise, they wouldn't be able to survive the night. They looked around and gathered some wood and combustible foliage; making a pyre. They only had to light the fire now, but there was nothing there they could do this with. They pondered for a while over the options, and the prospects were bleak. Suddenly, the friend came up with an idea. He suggested that Lal Shahbaz Qalandar transform himself into a falcon, and fetch some fire from hell. The Qalandar liked the proposition; he became a falcon and flew towards hell to procure fire. His friend waited in the desert for hours, his bones glueing together all for the aggressive chill in the air, but there was no sign of return. It was quite some time before the Qalandar came back. The friend rushed to him, hopeful, but was disappointed at not locating any fire with him.

Emphatically, he addressed the Qalandar, "You went to hell to get some fire so that we would warm ourselves up, but you have returned empty-handed!"

Lal Shahbaz Qalandar stopped for a minute and replied, "There is no fire in hell. Everyone who goes there brings their own fire, and pain, from this world."

Chapter One

THERE WERE thirteen gates to the old city of Lahore, though only some stood through the sands of time. Thirteen ways to get out of this damned place, Mehar always thought. She always believed - almost desperately - that one gate would open for her to leave these narrow alleyways and cluttered lanes one day. As a child, she would keep remembering the names of all the gates (Mochi and Mori would often be counted as one, and Sheranwaali too challenging to pronounce) and wonder which would prove to be lucky for her. Akbari? No, that had been torn down by the British. Probably Masti? Or Bhaati?

And then it happened. One day, a gate opened. She got married and left the Old City, hoping to never look back.

But as she returned to her house that day after being away for seven years - divorced and desolate - she marvelled at the naivety of her reasoning. For if there were thirteen ways to get out of this place, there were also thirteen demonic tangles to suck her back in.

Thirteen.

Should have known nothing good comes out of this number. Should have listened to one of her colleagues in the medical college. Should have looked at her past.

She paid the rickshaw driver after he helped her get the modest trunk out onto the road, where cars honked at each other in a clamorous procession. She dragged the trunk along, the part that grated against the ground producing tiny sparks of fire. She entered through the Delhi Gate and made her way inside, assaulted by the obscene cacophony of brimming life that was typical of the area, and passed the ancient Mughal mosque with a sense of defiance; pretending not to notice the numerous eyes that darted around in meaningless projectiles before locating her in their fields and getting locked on her. Her black burqa flowed in all directions in the strong wind, propelling her steps in the direction they were already on; nature was also a party to the vile scheme.

She hated the place all the more: its resilience to time secretly mocking her insides.

Old City, where nothing happened, nothing changed, nothing mattered.

Old City: nothing.

A place of nothingness where magnificent stories were carved out of oblivion.

She subconsciously boosted her pace and took a sharp turn after walking straight for a while. A shapeless, four-storey structure with an air of being constructed in haste abutted the central lane, dividing it into two. She stopped for a moment before the brawny wooden door that had given away at the sides, the chain dangling over it liable to break into a thousand little pieces for the rust that had possessed it in many decades. She knocked at it and looked above at the lofty structure with eerie dimensions that was her home.

But is home really a place? She thought.

She knocked again.

She waited.

Cursed. Evil. Slut.

Mehar.

* * *

In the periphery of Sukkur in Northern Sindh, amidst vast swathes of partially arable land which displayed crops of wheat and rice that gleamed in the sturdy sun, stood a mansion duly protected from public sight by *Amaltas* and Palm trees. The mansion was nestled in the farthest end of the sprawling estate, and the intricate architectural details of the mansion borrowed heavily from Talpur and Kalhora influences, even when its construction was somewhat recent.

The front door of the mansion opened with a start. Shabbaraat, who was already on his toes for the imminent arrival, took a moment to recognise his *sahabjee*, whose eyes were all puffy and whose lips cracked at the sides.

All rich people are naturally very ugly.

Money is such a saviour.

The other male members of the family and acquaintances had already gone to the annexe, which faced the mansion at an oblique angle. Shabbaraat looked at the guests through the open door, and then straightened his back to stand attentively in front of Feroze.

"Tea," Feroze ordered as he entered, more out of a habit to cement his authority than any actual need, the command in his voice palpable despite the grief.

That is what habitual denial does to you. It prevents you from being honest with others.

"Jee, *sahabjee*." Shabbaraat perkily moved to a side and ran to carry out his sahabjee's orders, feigning a well-rehearsed semblance of despondence. Barray Sahab, Hashmatullah Malik, had passed away a day ago - and Shabbaraat's only worry was if his new sahabjee would lay the staff off.

Feroze went straight to the study, his father's study, which apparently hadn't accepted the reality of its owner having passed away. Everything was as he had left it. On the study table, the dead man's half-smoked cigar jittered at the concept of life.

Who will smoke me now?

You? Are you your father? Does history repeat itself?

Feroze sank into a chair and closed his eyes.

Myasthenia Gravis. That was what had killed his father, but it was more convenient for Feroze to routinely surpass the details and tell everyone, "It was sudden." Hashmatullah had had the disease for many years, something he would always tell others to garnish his credentials. A success is a thing of joy, a success with disease is a thing of marvel. Medicines, taken regularly, had always kept the condition in check. But then something happened, and the nerves that supplied his father's breathing system went bad. He died because he couldn't breathe anymore.

What a terrible way to die, your body insidiously turning on itself. Self-immolation.

The ticking bomb had exploded. And the after-effects were shattering. Now that it had happened, it was difficult for Feroze to manoeuvre through the process. How do people write such exquisite obituaries, how do they simplify death?

Am I sad at my father's demise?

Terribly so.

Do I miss him?

It's complicated.

Feroze missed having his father around, the surety of security he provided, and the guarantee of the provision he carried, but being in his physical presence had never been easy for Feroze.

When Shabbaraat brought the tea, Feroze had snoozed off. He woke up by the sound of the servant's slippers being swept against the floor and gestured at him to put the cup on the study table, and leave Strangely enough, and before he knew it, Feroze's dismay soon gave way to an inexplicable sense of lightness. He tried to be in denial, for he would detest himself for clandestinely rejoicing at his father's death. Things anyway were proceeding too fast.

That is what habitual denial does to you. It prevents you from being honest with yourself.

Later, while sipping his tea and smoking a cigarette, Feroze found himself fixated on only one thing, oblivious to the fact that the staff of the mansion circled him momentarily and spoke in hushed tones about the similarities of the father and son. Does history repeat itself?

Death of the father.

Death.

The end of one thing.

The beginning of another?

He knew he had to call Bina. But with the chasm of so many wasted years between them, he did not know what to say. Was it surmountable? But everything has to start somewhere, like everything had to end somewhere.

Like death?

He waged hastily through his phone: no number.

Diaries, notebooks, laptop: none.

Was she on social media? Of course, she was something of a celebrity there. But she might never reply.

And then it hit him. If there was one person who would have Bina's number, it would be her.

Mehar.

* * *

Inside the Delhi Gate in Old Lahore, amidst a maze of passageways that became narrower as you progressed, life ruffled even in the late hours of the night. Men gathered in the clearings in the edge of the lanes to enjoy tobacco laden paan with their friends, discussing ideas on how to make money and how to score women. The women indulged in conversations with their peers across their windows that stood high on the two sides of the lanes. They casually confided in each other what filthy swines their husbands and lovers were. In a lane, a little off the fabled Mughal mosque, stood a four-storied house built ages ago, though layers of construction were evidently added to it later. On the top of the wooden door that opened into the street, the name of the original owner, "Satnam Singh," wasn't legible anymore - both because it had faded away in almost a century and because it was written in Gurmukhi, and the current residents of the area rarely knew the script. Three people were present inside the house; one of them had just returned there earlier that day.

When Mehar's phone rang, she was half asleep. She was spent dealing with the unwelcome notes her brother and sister-in-law had made at her and came up to her room on the fourth floor of the house. Mehar looked at the name flashing on the phone from the corner of her eye.

Aariz.

She shut her eyes and parted the lids slowly to let any doubt away.

Aariz.

If there was one man in the world she could talk to at that point, it was him. But right then, there wasn't even one man in this world she wanted to talk to, or even a woman for that matter. She let the call die, and cupped her phone still in bed. There were three missed calls by Feroze. She was surprised; they had never talked over the phone before, albeit they clearly knew each other. Their connecting string was a woman they both were fond of - in very different ways.

Bina Vankwani.

Everything that Mehar was not.

Not cursed. Not evil. Not slut.

The lovely, vibrant Bina.

Mehar had an immediate desire to call Bina right then. Where was she? Was she fine? Had she adjusted to her new life? It had been more than a year since the women hadn't talked. There was a time in medical college these two had been practically inseparable, much to the surprise of all. They were polarised, two people coming from completely different worlds - the connection they shared was designed by a string that was impossible for others to see. It wasn't goodwill or friendship, though that came later.

Maybe it was angst; maybe it was anger.

It could have been sympathy as well.

Mehar got up slowly from the bed, as if any swift movement of her body parts would startle the air around her, and the delicate shards her life had been reduced to would come tumbling down upon her. Scratching her, tearing her. She would start bleeding from parts of her body that had already turned blue after having run out of blood.

But she wouldn't scream.

Mehar's room, a compact, scrawny structure added to a dying building in haste and need, opened into a small balcony that sat atop the intersection of two alleys below. In the years she had been away, the room had been converted into a store. Discarded pieces from her sister-in-law, Shama's dowry decorated the room in a wayward fashion. Mehar made her way through the clutter, jumping atop a rolled rug, hitting a dysfunctional sewing machine with her toe whose nail lost the connection with the underlying skin, and a warm liquid oozed out.

But she wouldn't scream.

She parted the net curtains at the entrance of the balcony, unlocked the glass door that grated meekly on opening, and came out into the open. She seated herself on the broken chair that monsoon rains and Lahore's dust had joined in an unholy alliance to create an eerie art of. The chair creaked as she sat on it, but it worked for her all the same. Mehar inserted her hand in the pocket of her shalwar and, after a few advances, found what she was looking for: a Capstan cigarette pack. She took out a cigarette, lit it, and inhaled as if her life depended on it. She exhaled; a microcosm of carbon dioxide and arsenic escaped her lips and shadowed everything around her. The smoke accelerated through the thick Lahore air, hovered for a while in the halo of existence around her, and then descended upon the people walking in the lanes below on either side of her. It was strangely liberating, this act of smoking, now that what she associated with it was no more around to hit her, beat her, mock her.

Cursed. Evil. Slut.

She felt a tinge of shooting pain in her flank right then, her body playing funny tricks on her. The leather belts had been her frequent associates during the past years, but there was no physical injury anymore.

This pain was a hoax.

Wasn't everything?

Ghost limb syndrome, she recalled from her medical studies.

"Scream, you bitch!" he used to bellow as leather hit her soft skin; the thud reverberating through her body in an agonising current.

She whimpered. She bit her lips. She shivered.

But she wouldn't scream.

This infuriated him all the more. The hits got stronger, the force multiplied. She got used to them, accepting them as a ritualistic rite of marriage. Like sex. He would stop when he was exhausted, furious at having failed to make her scream again. But God knows he never stopped trying.

Ahmad was sure he would break Mehar one day; there was nothing more insulting to his masculinity than her negation to scream. But he didn't know that in the place Mehar came from, people were born with certain qualities. They were survivors; they lived through almost everything that came their way: war, famine, disease, violence, and belts. The resilience of those walls and lanes that had survived centuries of warfare and plundering was a genetic attribute of the people born in this place.

She took a long drag. The nicotine entered her blood and contracted her lungs, allowing only the amount of oxygen that she needed. She wasn't used to excesses anyway.

Just then, she heard it. The music. An old Bollywood song being played from a distant neighbour's house, carried over ever so melodiously by the waves of the night air.

"Khoya khoya chand,
Khula Asmaan,

Ankhon mein saari raat jaiyegi,
Tum ko bhi kaisay neend aayegi?"

She hated this place, but for a moment, her revulsion gave way to nostalgia. One out of the thirteen gates opened and brought in a flurry of memories. Happier times? She wasn't sure, but less complicated times.

Her phone rang again at that point; she muted it to avoid the squall being caused to the music.

She didn't check who it was calling this time.

She lit another cigarette.

Chapter Two

BINA LEFT the operation theatre, groggy after standing for four hours during an operative procedure and putting all her muscles to good use. Her scrubs were splattered with blood and pus, and her right upper arm hurt slightly from the excessive force she had to devote to the retractor. Her colleagues often joked that she wasn't suited to be in this department with her thin, long frame. "One day," they joked, "You will dislocate your own shoulder while fixing someone else's." She went to the doctor's changing room, disrobed, and flung the scrubs in a carton of dirty laundry, which would be taken for sterilisation later. She changed into a pair of jeans and a loose cotton shirt and left the premises for the short walk to her room in the doctor's hostel where she lived. The air was pleasant; the weather of Islamabad was always a source of joy for those who lived here; the Margalla Hills routinely sealed neat packets of fresh, cool air and threw it towards the people dwelling at its base. She passed the cafeteria and the grounds, where frantic attendants of the patients lay on the ground and supplicated, praying for the recovery of whoever it was they were with.

Despicable places, these hospitals!

Bina knew her walk would accompany the usual string of thoughts in her head, even the music in her headphones rarely muffled these. But it did not bother her anymore; she had accepted it as just a routine play that was unveiled in her head on every emergency night shift. It rang in her mind, not like mind-boggling life questions, but like a piece of background music.

Track one: Nusrat Fateh Ali Khan.

Track two: Abida Parveen.

Track three: Bina's reverie.

Why did I choose a field that is typically a male field?

Why did I choose to leave Sindh and Punjab to settle here?

Where do I go from here?

But the answers came to her as automatically as the questions did. And they were quite straightforward; it was all because of who she was. The defiant, rebellious Bina! Some people are not meant to live only their own lives; they are saddled with the cumulative baggage of many around them. Bina had convinced herself that she was made to always be in motion, regardless of what came her way. She had to rise above everything, especially the things it was deemed she would not be able to rise against. She had to swim through tornados and hurricanes.

Like Bhulan?

Bina tried to delete the thought immediately. The fear of tragedy aroused distastefully in her gut at the thought of Bhulan, the blind dolphins that lived in Indus near her home.

Sukkur.

Another world, another age...

As Bina neared the door of her apartment on the second floor of the hostel, her phone started buzzing. She had told Papa a hundred times not to wait for her call, that her timings were unscheduled and he should just sleep, but Papa never listened. It was hard enough for him already that Bina was away, he would say, and it was essential for him to listen to Bina's voice or else he couldn't sleep. She took the phone out of her jeans pocket, dreading if it was a call for a post-operative emergency instead of Papa. But as she saw the name, life seeped out of her body. She stood petrified as if she had seen an apparition. It was neither Papa nor the emergency department. The name roared from the screen, casting a spell on Bina, almost tormenting her. She did not know how to react. The call was coming from one thousand kilometres south of where she was, and it had been many years since she had heard his voice.

She wanted to hear the voice desperately. She also wanted to silence the voice forever.

Time stood between her and her phone like a wall, insurmountable, carrying memories of the indefensible.

And then, in a moment of waning lucidity, she took the call.

"Bina!" the voice would have been a shriek had it not been a sigh.

There was silence from her side.

"Bina, I know you're there. *Keinya aahein tun?*"

How have you been?

She hated herself for the flutter that ran through her heart. Should someone call emergency?

"Feroze," she started, "how are you?"

Silence.

She thought the conversation was over, so she made an effort, "I heard about uncle. I'm sorry."

But was she?

"Yes, it was sudden. But we are doing fine. Amma is still in shock, though. You tell me about yourself. It has been so long."

"Ten years."

"Eleven years."

"Yeah."

"Bina, I have meant to call you for a long time. I'm very sorry."

He was. But for whom?

"You don't need to be sorry, Feroze. I guess we got very busy. Anyway, are you in Sukkur? How did you get my number?"

A stupid question, and she wasn't the one to be asking these. Her number was on the doctors' list on every rota in every ward of her hospital. It was also on the websites of the communities and NGOs she was a part of.

"Yes, I am in Sukkur. Where are you? I got your number from Mehar. She told me you have shifted to Islamabad."

"Oh, Mehar. Poor girl. She got divorced after living with that vile excuse of a husband for seven years. But I'm happy she got rid of him. She should have done it sooner."

Bina regretted revealing Mehar's personal details as she said this; these two people had rarely met. But it is always easier to talk about other people when you don't know what to talk about.

"I didn't know that. I'm sorry."

He was. For her.

"Yeah, well. Unfortunate things happen to us."

The "us" came out a bit too loud.

"Have you completed your degree? You must have. Are you working?"

"Yes, I am."

"Bina, are you still mad at me for what happened? You know it wasn't my fault."

She stopped for a second. She had feared this moment and was putting up a perfect show of pretending that they could end this conversation without bringing it up. She also knew that it wasn't his fault; she wasn't sure if she blamed him for being an accomplice to what happened or for failing her. The shrieks of a girl belled in her head; rage followed. She thought about inserting her hand in the phone to grab his vocal cords and pull them out to strangle his neck with.

"I know it wasn't."

"Can we meet?"

Silence.

"Bina! Where are you?"

Silence.

And then, "Feroze, goodbye!"

"Bina! Bina! Bina!…"

But the phone had gone dead.

When he tried to call her again, his number had been blocked.

* * *

The Allama Iqbal International Airport in Lahore is seemingly obvious for its lack of activity for the country's second largest city. It's almost a dull sight, and the vision on display after passing through hefty security checks is disappointing. While the international departures lounge springs to life during the late hours of the night, as all major international carriers operate during that time, the domestic affairs teem with sluggish activity throughout the hours. The most considerable commotion is at the parking; people insisting on parking their cars in the drop lane and the ensuing brawls with the airport staff are a constant sight.

Bina had been used to these. She passed by a passenger bargaining the rate with the loader and smiled. Someone was always out to loot someone. She had left the city after completing her medical degree but had missed how loud and obnoxious Lahore was: a megacity that was still an overgrown village.

She was late; she knew he would already be waiting. And he was.

* * *

Twenty-five minutes ago, Aariz was removing his hand carry from the plane's compartment, the usual push and pull of a Pakistani flight already in motion. People had lined up to leave the plane even while the hostess shouted - first politely, then angrily, then tearfully - at them to wait, but they were already shoving their elbows in all the bodily parts of others they could secure access to. The flight from Dubai was a blink-and-miss affair, but he hadn't taken the flight for a long time. But this time, he had to come. He could feel the stale warmth of Lahore's air already, even when the doors of the plane hadn't yet opened to let the place in. He still wasn't sure if coming to Pakistan was a good idea, but it was already too late for such conjecture. He had informed only Bina of his arrival and guessed if she would be at the airport.

He smiled. She would be late.

The practical, I-mean-business-Bina would have been caught up in a last-minute assignment, a dying patient, or a fight with someone over her rights.

The fights-and-rights Bina.

Some things never change.

* * *

Bina looked at Aariz as she approached him, standing out in the crowd of people jumpily meeting their waiting relatives. He looked as handsome as ever; the age still hadn't started telling on him. His body was still taut as if he was in his twenties, and wore his half-sleeved T-shirt well. His complexion was still untouched by the blemishes of time. He had always been a good-looking fellow, at least after puberty hit him, Bina would joke, and would tell him it was the first thing people noticed about him. He knew. His complexion had often led people to ask him if he hailed from the Northern Areas of the country, his eyes a lighter-than-average shade of brown, a tuft of thick hair always sitting neatly upon a symmetrical face. Two cheekbones erupted furiously at the sides, and a strong chin carried the featherlight load of two thin lips. His build was medium; it retained an athletic quality even when he was sedentary.

Bina advanced towards him, envying how age had refused to mark itself on him.

But the eyes were different.

They had lost any depth. It was as if they were hollow. Like a camera's lens.

Or maybe, they were always like this, and she hadn't noticed. They had always been so engaged in garrulous conversations, that they rarely found the time to dissect the other's external appearances, which clearly did not matter anyway.

Bina strode towards him, poking him with her thumb to get

his attention which was focused elsewhere.

"Aariz, my Benjamin Button!" she hugged him warmly, her smile touching her ears.

Aariz held her and replied, "Miss B! How's my favourite doctor doing? Are you giving your patients medicines or lectures?"

He let his grip loose on Bina, who backed out to look at Aariz's luggage. She caught him looking at her, gleaming.

The smile was also different. As if it were plastered on the face.

Aariz had a small bag, and he pushed it along as they walked towards her car. Bina wanted to ask him if he had come only for a week given the lack of luggage, but realised Aariz always worked in his own ways.

"Don't start complaining about the heat, Aariz. Every year now, we have a new heatwave coming. We think we've seen the worst, but every year comes with its own strategy of breaking the records."

"I am coming from a desert, Bina. I have become half a camel already."

Neither spoke much during the short journey from the arrivals' lounge to the parking, but both were happy to be in each other's company. As they sat in their car, Aariz looked at Bina and asked, "So what type of doctor are you becoming?"

"An orthopaedic surgeon, Aariz," she growled, knowing what his answer would be.

"I always knew you had a pedo in you."

She shook her head. Always the wrong jokes.

As the car's engine sprang to life, Aariz busied himself with the car's stereo.

"You will not find much here, Aariz," Bina interrupted. "You know what I listen to, Sufi, classical and folk."

"Even your choice in music is a cliche, B!"

Bina, finding the parking receipt that had to be returned at the exit, didn't look at him while responding, "I am sure your guilty pleasure is Justin Bieber."

The car accelerated and went out into the evening, leaving behind a hyper group of thirty people dancing in the air with garlands in their hands - some were making tiktoks, others were taking selfies - it was still some ten minutes before the flight from Jeddah arrived.

They drove in silence for a while. Aariz looked at the new multi-storeyed constructions that weren't there the last time he was here. By the time they passed the Army checkpoint leading to the Cantonment, Nayyara Noor had concluded her rendition of a famous poem by Faiz.

"Though I wished, the breach of heart did not allow,

To share grievances, after the formalities."

It was either the effect of the words or the natural progression of events that Aariz said, "Bina, I am not really sure why I came back."

"Neither am I. I would not have come back if I were you."

"Is someone finally losing hope?"

"Not for myself, at least."

* * *

About half an hour later, they were seated in a cafe in Gulberg, waiting for their coffees.

"Aariz, it's almost like the old times."

"Do you miss them?"

"Don't you?"

"Hmm."

"I am only in Lahore for a conference on knee replacement, Aariz. The stars really love you, making it convenient to give you a free chauffeur when you need one."

"I wouldn't have paid with the driving skills you have."

Bina made a face. She knew her driving style wasn't the most genteel.

"So, what has been happening in your life, Bina?"

"Aariz, we talked only three days ago. Don't pretend we need to catch up."

"Yeah, but audio calls don't let me see the change of your expressions when you talk, and let's be honest, they change by the second."

"I understand where you are coming from. Must be difficult having a face carved in stone."

"You can do better than that, Bina!"

"Of course, I can, but I adjust it according to the calibre of my audience."

"Ouch, you've learnt from the best!"

"If that helps you sleep at night."

It was only after they had gulped down their cappuccinos that they started having a real conversation.

"So, how are uncle and aunty doing?"

"They are doing fine, Aariz. Though I know they both secretly wish I return to Sukkur. Papa is vocal about it. Ma just prays for my change of heart."

"Do you plan on doing so?"

"No, Aariz. I cannot quit my training mid-way. And I like working in Islamabad. There's no way I could have had the same exposure back home. In fact, we are trying to convince our parents to move to Karachi. Rinkle and her husband also shifted there after their marriage."

"I see. And what are their views about this?"

"Papa is reluctant. He doesn't think he can ever let go of Sukkur. Ma is almost neutral on this. Remember I told you how she's fixated on going to Balochistan for the Hinglaj pilgrimage? I don't think she ever plans on doing that, but that is something she has retained in her life to look forward to, especially now that both her daughters are independent. So sometimes she's like, *yeah, Karachi will be nearer to Hingol, so it's a good idea.* But she keeps on flipping."

"Right," Aariz smiled, "And how's work?"

"Painfully exhausting, but I enjoy it. How's yours?"

"Mine? Well, you know it's not regular. It's on a project-by-project basis. But allows me to travel at will, and not be another member of Club Corporate Slavery."

"Damn, I like how rich people like you put up such a show of it," Bina laughed.

"Well, I am not rich. Feroze is."

The dynamics of the scene changed immediately as the name of Feroze was taken. Suddenly, a sense of gravity befell the two friends. Aariz regretted not having been more careful. The previously chatty Bina now carried a solemn expression.

"Aariz, I have to tell you something."

"That you have a crush on me that you've hidden all these years?" Aariz tried to lighten things up, but he knew his attempt was lame.

"Shut up," Bina forced a laugh. "I'd rather die with my cats than fall for you. You still have that impish sense of humour."

"Works every time."

"Yeah, right. So…"

On seeing lines cross her brow, Aariz's countenance changed to that of concern.

"What is it?" He extended his hand. She almost held it before withdrawing hers.

"Feroze called me, three days ago." She paused, "After eleven years."

"Oh." Aariz stayed silent for a moment, unsure whether there was nothing to be said or too much.

"I blocked his number."

"Well, if that is what you think is right. I haven't been in touch with him for a long time."

"Yeah, I guessed that."

"You know his father died, right?"

"Yeah, I saw it on Twitter. I thought about leaving him a message, but something came up, and I totally forgot about it."

"Hmmm…"

"Bina, are you doing fine?"

"Yes, I am, Aariz. Thank you for asking. I'm sure I will have closure soon."

"How many closures will we seek?" He tried to laugh, before realising the joke hadn't gone well with either of them.

"Aariz, we need to go see Mehar. It's been a year since I haven't seen her."

Mehar.

His heart missed a beat. Something about this woman had captivated him since he had known her. But the stage wasn't set here by biology like it usually is. It was something he couldn't know.

"She got divorced."

"Oh."

Oh.

A safe word.

Doesn't give away too much.

"Let's meet her then. I am here for a while."

"I missed you, Aariz. I am so glad you are here."

"So am I."

Neither needed a polygraph test to know that he was partly lying.

Chapter Three

"FROM ALLAH, we come, and to Allah, we return."

Rasm-e-Qul: the third - and final - day of mourning according to Islamic tradition. People from a particular belt of northern Sindh, the late Hashmatullah's constituency, had driven in hordes to attend the ritual for the peace of the departed soul. And then there were others: people with power, people with money, people with favours to give, people with favours to seek. The men sat in the outer drawing room of the mansion, careful not to ruin their freshly starched shalwar kameez. They inquired Feroze about the cause of Hashmatullah's death, but their attention spans waned steeply while listening to the answer Feroze was giving on repeat. They said a few fervent lines about how great their late leader was, and how much he had done for the area despite not *fully* belonging here, before venturing off to more pressing topics like the political scenario of the country and the future of the Sindhi nationalist parties in the coming years. Some people brought ajraks for Feroze to formally proclaim him as the heir of the legacy.

Legacy.

The burden of legacy.

The sins of the father.

Feroze had inherited both. While others simply awed at the size of the mansion and fleet of cars that adorned its driveway, and approvingly nodded at each other - half-envying, half-hating Feroze given he was the sole heir of all of this - no one noticed the ghosts of the past that Feroze had inherited collaterally. Probably not even Feroze, right then.

The women sat inside the mansion, in the lounge with Italian frescoes and Belgian crystals - carefully handpicked by his mother at each of her European trips. "In Belgium," she often told Feroze, carrying him around her choicest collection, "there's a crystal festival held every year, though no one knows when it will be held. When your father and I went for the first time to the country, we got lucky, and it was held right before the day we were leaving. Just don't ask me about the trouble we had while carrying all this stuff back home." She would end the story with a flicker of her hand and smirk that ended midway in its natural course.

The women grouped in the lounge, counting their date seeds as they prayed on these.

Tick. Tick. Tick.

The seeds fell upon each other, forming a mound that continued to augment in size. An hourglass that was bringing all present nearer to their deaths as well—three seconds gone.

The women who inspired protocol were seated on the sofas (from France) that circled the room's periphery. They gesticulated their sorrow by intricate choreography of their hands, the gold on their arms clinking as they spoke. One cursed her designer under her breath for not readying her outfit on time. Most women were hunched on the floor, centring around a mammoth crystal structure (from Belgium). It wasn't the prettiest of things: a woman with her mouth open and snakes slithering upon her head.

"It's a Gorgon," his mother would tell a young Feroze. "In Greek mythology, there are three Gorgons: Medusa, Stheno, and Euryale, though I don't know which one this is. They symbolise safety and protection. And don't ask me about its price; it cost us a fortune."

She always skipped telling him that the Gorgons would turn

everyone who looked at them into stones. They turned silent forever.

The women stole glances upon the ghastly statue amidst the sound of tick, tick, tick and sneered at its presence. Some had stopped praying as they were sure nothing would be accepted by divinity with such symbols of heresy in the house. At least they could have covered this horrible woman with a cloth; there has been a death in the family. For all practical purposes, they were only dropping the seeds to the ground.

Tick. Tick. Tick.

The dance of life.

"They don't even have an *Ayat Ul Kursi* hanging in this room," one woman whispered to another.

"I have heard there are two hundred rooms in this house," said another.

***

Feroze hadn't slept properly since the night his father was declared dead. It was partly because of the social obligations - people came thronging in at all times of the day to console him, reminding him what a great man his father was before slipping him a note about someone who had to be obliged, and partly because there was in motion an emotional upheaval in his gut.

If death really was the end of one thing and the beginning of another, he couldn't know where to place the distinction.

He didn't know where to draw the line.

Line.

Bina could say something about lines.

Bina, he remembered. She had blocked his number, and Mehar had also ignored all his calls since the only one she received and gave him Bina's number.

Eleven years.

Eleven centuries.

What is surmountable and what is not?

Who could say?

Feroze tried to sleep, he lay in his bed for two hours, but there was too much in his mind that could not be silenced. Which was a first; words were a rarity in his house, silence wasn't.

He got up, giving up on his hope of getting some shut-eye, and went towards his father's study on the ground floor. The lights were on in the main lounge. Clearly, Shabbaraat wasn't doing an outstanding job of managing things. He descended the stairs softly, careful not to wake his mother, who had been inconsolable and Feroze was too tired to pander to. He entered the study, its grand wooden door creaking only very slightly, and turned the lights on.

The study sprang to life, and the chandelier's light was directly reflected from the showcase behind the study table on which his father displayed his cherished collection of spirits and wines, even though he drank only occasionally. The exquisite bottles of Johnnie Walker and Chivas Regal greeted Feroze through their glass cage.

Feroze looked at the study with a sense of derision. It was as if it had also denied accepting what had happened, like his mother.

This was where Hashmatullah spent most of his time when he was home, which was not often. It would host his friends, his affiliates, and sometimes his foes; there weren't any permanent friends or enemies in politics anyway. Two walls of the study were covered entirely with book laden shelves, dusted every second day. The third wall had a window and his father's study table before a cellar, and the fourth one carried pictures of his father.

He started by observing the pictures. Everyone said he resembled his father. He used to be proud of it while not wholly subscribing to these opinions. He wanted to be like him. He wanted to be him.

But want is a strange thing. You can never know what it is that you truly want for yourself and what you internalise that others want for you.

Where one ends, and the other begins.

A difficult line to draw.

Bina!

Feroze went over to the corner shelf, overlooking the textbook collections his father had; there were some books he would find in all of his father's friends' libraries as well:

The Men Who Ruled India by Philip Mason.

Why Nations Fail by James Robinson.

Shahabnaama by Qudrat Ullah Shahab.

Friends, Not Masters by Ayub Khan.

Daughter of the East by Benazir Bhutto.

My Feudal Lord by Tehmina Durrani.

He extended his hand towards the drawer his father was conscientious about. He opened it and took out the diary. It was his grandfather's recollections of a time that wasn't Feroze's. Of a time that underscored so much of what happened in their lives.

The Pity of Partition by Ayesha Jalal fell to the floor as Feroze shut the drawer with a thud. Feroze picked it up and stuffed it in an empty corner.

While leaving the study, something caught the edge of Feroze's eye.

His father's half-smoked cigar, lying on the study table.

Who will smoke me now?

I will.

He picked it up and hastened towards his room. The Gorgon looked at him as he walked past the lounge.

Gorgon, who made people stone.

Gorgon, who made people silent.

Feroze would never realise that perhaps the heaviest inheritance he was to carry all his life would be silence.

* * *

Feroze lit the cigar and carried it to his lips. He wished it would somehow smell of his father so that he could bid farewell to his smell as well, and the ritual of saying the final goodbye could be complete, but it only smelled of aromatic tobacco. If he could exhale his father through his system, wouldn't that be liberating? Unknowingly, he imitated his father's smoking style, carrying it delicately between his fingers, the index finger rounded, the middle straight forwards. He liked the taste; he coughed.

Right then, Shabbaraat passed the lawns below Feroze's window, and caught sight of the room on the upper story shrouded in the dark of the night, but visible for the parted curtains and the light that shone inside. It hit him, the similarity, the same style, the same build, and he thought he had never registered it when Hashmatullah was alive.

Shahbaraat observed him silently for a while, not knowing where the father ended and the son began.

Chapter Four

AARIZ ENTERED his apartment, and was hit by the forgotten familiarity of the place. He had lived here for about eight years, and it was still redolent of the numerous bittersweet memories he made during that period of transition of his life. A cosy, two-bedroom place near Gulberg located on the fifth floor, Aariz had moved here soon after he turned eighteen. Old Papa had left him a fortune after his death, but it took Aariz quite some years to reach the age of inheritance. For the most part, Aariz had been the only inhabitant of the apartment, even though visits from his and Old Papa's friends were frequent. For the initial two years of living here, Aariz remained steady, busying himself with college. Afterwards, he started travelling extensively, enrolled in an online Masters programme from an American University, and the apartment often remained empty. It had been four years since he shifted to Dubai, and visits to Pakistan weren't frequent.

Not that anyone was waiting for him here.

Not that he wanted to be here.

But Dubai was also a temporary resort for him, and he stayed for months on end in other countries. But if the flow of rent determines your place of residence, then it was Dubai for Aariz. He had established a consultancy firm there and could afford the option of living what Bina called the good life.

Aariz tried to turn the lights on, but the switchboard had caved in. The place was damp; a coat of dust had overtaken the colour of the furniture. The ceiling laced with spider-webs, and the glass on the windows had become grey. He put his luggage to a side, and took out his phone to call *khaala*, the house help who had worked with them when Old Papa was alive and later when Aariz shifted here.

"Khaala, *salam*. Aariz here. I have come back to Pakistan."

"Aariz, *mera bacha*. How are you? I missed you so much," Khaala started crying; the factory that produced her tears was always gainfully employed.

"Khaala, can you come to work for me? I need help with my house."

"*Beta*, I cannot walk anymore. This bloody diabetes, I tell you. They say they might have to cut my foot, those savages. But my daughter Zainab is free, she can come to work. I'll send her tomorrow."

Aariz expressed his concern about her ailment, and thanked her.

"Aariz *beta* will pay my daughter in dollars now, as he is a foreign Babu," Khaala said before cutting the phone.

Aariz went over to the window and opened it; that afforded a pleasant view of the city, the vista it offered was often touted by his friends as their favourite feature of the apartment; especially because high-rise apartments weren't very common in Lahore. He leaned against the sill, and thought about what had happened when he used to live in this city. How he couldn't process it in the beginning, how he had gotten used to it, and how he blamed himself for it years afterwards. He tasted blood in his mouth; he spat. It had been years he hadn't met his step-parents. He had no idea if they were alive. Aariz had cut off all bonds with them as soon as his age allowed him the option.

He never looked back, and neither did they.

Sometimes, things can end just like that. In a blink, a nano-second, it's as if they never existed.

The last Aariz heard about them was that they had given birth to a son. Aariz had a step-brother he would never meet in his life.

His real father, Old Papa, was a man of many words and friends. Some of his friends had helped Aariz start his new life. They were an assortment of all kinds: lawyers, doctors, journalists, writers, and government servants. He would have to meet so many of them, he thought.

This time Aariz had come to Pakistan for a consultancy service that was tendered to his firm; he had made quite a reputation for himself in the field of architecture. He had to tell Bina he had come to meet her as well, and that could've been a reason, but Aariz wasn't sure.

He wasn't sure about a lot of things.

Because surety espouses a set of balanced, sensible ground to work on, but nothing made sense to him. Nothing had made sense to him for years. If it ever did, and he convinced himself it must have when Old Papa was alive, he did not remember it anymore. His level of detachment was soaring incessantly, and he wasn't sure whether it was his innate modus operandi or a defence mechanism. He waded through life like a water-proof chemical that pervaded everything but absorbed nothing. Like a layer of oil suspended upon water. But this didn't stop him from functing perfectly. In fact, he functioned better than most. To trick his mind into pumping adrenaline and dopamine, he immersed himself in all experiences at times a bit too strongly. He could very well pull off a meticulous show of everything.

Everything was a performance anyway.

And no one could ever guess that the handsome, successful, funny, smart Aariz was made of different clay. It was as if he looked at his own life from an exterior angle.

His life was his theatre.

He was the actor, and the audience.

He returned to the sitting area and started sifting through some of his belongings that lay around: half-read books, dirty laundry, discarded equipment - it was a mess. He stumbled upon a picture that he held for a while.

Old mama and old Papa.

It was before Aariz was born.

Old mama had died during his birth.

For him.

What a waste.

She gave birth to a body.

Did she forget to transfer the soul?

They were smiling in the picture, as if at Aariz. But why would they smile at him? Was this collection of bones, muscles, and skin worthy of being smiled at?

Aariz wanted to take in the picture and cry. He wanted to feel sadness, loss, grief, anything.

He did not.

Nothing made sense to him.

Not grief.

Not loss.

But even in this state of senselessness, memories came jolting down in Aariz's mind. Like they always did on seeing Old Papa. And with it came the concept of age. Everything had an age, as Old Papa would tell him. And for Aariz, the idea of age blended with the identity of things. Not that age distinguished anything, but it was an essential qualification that Aariz depended upon to understand things better.

* * *

"Papa, what is the age of the universe?"

"It's 14 billion years, *beta.*"

"How many zeros are in a billion?"

"Nine."

And as a nine-year-old Aariz would start counting the zeros on his fingers, neatly placing every billion of the universe's history on one of his fingers, Old Papa would laugh. He would look at Aariz and start their favourite story: of the cosmos. Aariz never knew where the concept of the universe ended and that of the cosmos began. Still, he pretended to get what Old Papa said, deeming an extraordinary sense of interest in the topic.

"Above and beyond what we can feel, Aariz, there's this great unknown. You know the names of the planets, right? So there are planets, suns, moons, stars, and a wide variety of things that we have only recently begun to know about. When you grow up, you'll realise that we occupy an insignificant, almost oblivious place in the greater scheme of things. We don't know the expanse of time and space."

Aariz, still perplexed about this complicated idea that he had heard about before, would only revert to his original fixation: the age.

"What is the age of our planet, papa?"

"It's more than 4 billion years."

"So there was no Earth before that?"

"We cannot say, Aariz. About what was and what wasn't. Maybe it also existed before that, but in a different form. Things change their forms, and take on a new dimension of existence. We may not be able to feel it, not even know it, but it's an interesting concept."

The child's brain sped up to not lose track of the conversation.

"So, you are nine years old. The universe is 14 billion years old. But if you look at both these things now, like how we rewind your movies, they seem the same. That's the peculiar thing about time; it all comes down to be the same when it's gone."

"Do dead people become stars, papa?" Aariz shifted to a more manageable stream of intellectual conversation.

"Not really, beta," Old Papa would smile, "but they do in Lion King." On this question, Old Papa would always do his imitation of Mufasa, biting at Aariz's leg playfully.

"The universe is really old, then, Papa. We die when we get old.

Why hasn't it died?"

"As I said, things change their forms. Things do not continue in the same way as we know them. One thing emerges into another, and then maybe another. That's the beauty of life, *beta*. The fact that we don't know so much only makes it all the more interesting."

"What will I become when I die, papa?"

"What if I die before?"

"Papa, you're not answering."

"Remember, Aariz, no matter which forms we exist in, whether we're alive or dead, you will always be the joy of my heart, the light of my eyes. The cosmos will not change it ever."

"Then why will your cosmos change us into dead people?"

"Because it's the design of the cosmos, Aariz. And the cosmos works in peculiar ways."

* * *

To talk about the real reason for Aariz's return to the country, even the consultancy wasn't it; his work was going well abroad, and there had been numerous offers from Pakistan before that he had downrightly refused.

The consultancy was regarding the conservation of the Walled City of Lahore. The government had taken up a project to renovate the lanes and streets of the Old Lahore surrounding the Wazir Khan Masjid to be converted into a specimen that could be awed at. Preserving history. Generating revenue.

Aariz did not really care about the Walled City or its conservation. He didn't care about most things and would admit it even to himself in moments of extreme weakness coupled with honesty.

But he cared about something.

Or at least was enchanted by it.

The Walled City of Lahore.

Mehar.

It had been some years since he and Mehar had first met, through a formal introduction by Bina. The girls had been in medical college then. At first, Mehar did not strike Aariz as extraordinarily special.

There are six million women in the city of Lahore.

And she was another one of them.

But over time, they developed an uneasy friendship. In real life, it was always chaperoned by Bina; Mehar wouldn't meet him alone. But that lasted only a while because Mehar quit medical college in her third year, and went off to marry someone. That was it for their face-to-face contact. Virtually though, they would share a few texts now and then. Mehar's texts spoke to Aariz: they formed sounds and voices he could hear. This texting ritual continued even after Mehar's marriage, even if it reduced significantly in frequency. She wasn't in a happy marriage, Bina had told him that much, but Mehar would never.

She would never complain, never indulge personal details, never confide in him.

She would also never scream, but Aariz did not know that.

This strength that Mehar transpired held Aariz. He was not sure what to make of it. Were they made of the same clay? Were they figments of the same soul split in half?

Enigma.

Her mystery was what Aariz was attracted to.

In a world where conformance was the norm, Aariz's interest was piqued by those who stood apart.

There are six million women in the city of Lahore.

And then there's Mehar.

Chapter Five

MEHAR CAME out into the night, and stood still near the edge of the balcony, placing her hand lightly on the railing so the plaster wouldn't fall off, as it had done from so many places. The night embraced her, with the quintessential warmth it carries when it is laden with human activity. Below in the streets, canopies set up hurriedly in a wayward sequence hampered her view, but the 500-watt bulbs, managed by adept, sly connections between electric wires and set up every few meters, gave away light that formed a blazed trail as far as she could look. Policemen stood at every intersection by the fences and barricades they had set up, exhausted and at the sole clemency of the people around to offer them food. It was Mehar's first Muharram in Old Lahore where she wasn't actively involved with the process, setting up stalls offering water and sherbet to the passers-by and preparing *niyaaz* with the neighbourhood women. From the direction of the grand haveli that served as the epicentre of the processions every Islamic new year, a speaker's emphatic voice duly intertwined with wails waded through the air and moved everyone it made its way to.

This was their festival of mourning.

"The little Ali Asghar's throat had gone dry. Bibi Sakina came running to her father, 'Baba, come and see Asghar. He keeps crying. Can you get him some water?' As the Imam went, he saw that his son had even stopped crying, all for being parched. The Imam took his little son in his arms, and went near the edge of Euphrates, guarded by the enemy soldiers. 'He has done you no harm. He's only six months old', he pleaded with them to allow water to his son. Some enemy soldiers started crying on witnessing this sorry state of the Prophet's family. Ya Allah, what had the world become?"

There was silence. Everyone in the area had heard the story myriad times before. Mehar knew what would come next, but like the other people, she feared the following line. Does feigning ignorance change a fact? This silence was their way of trying to change history.

"And then came an arrow from Hurmala's bow. It hit the infant throat, piercing it, and the young prince breathed his last. The Imam cried, shaken, and took the lifeless body of his son to his chest."

There were wails; people cried as if it were a personal tragedy, and shouted slogans of "Ya Hussain, Ya Hussain!" The effect of this narration wasn't lost on them in all these centuries.

"The Imam kissed the boy and said, 'From Allah, we come, and to Allah, we return' seven times.

He went to his wife and told her, 'O Umme Rubab, you have to do what no mother should ever be supposed to do.' They buried their son's body together, in the burning sand of Karbala. Sakina stood by and cried."

"Ya Hussain, ya Hussain!"

"Later, some water reached the tents. Bibi Zainab offered it to Sakina, 'You are the youngest here. You start'. Sakina took the water and stood up to leave. The Bibi asked her where she was going, to which Sakina replied. 'To my brother, Ali Asghar. He is younger than me, and has been thirsty for three days.'"

Everyone wept. In Karbala - and Old Lahore.

"By the middle of the afternoon of 10th Muharram, the speaker continued, "all were martyred, even Abbas, Sakina's dear uncle who had done to get water for her as the children cried 'Al Atash, Al Atash', we are thirsty. Only the Imam remained, and his eldest son was too sick to walk."

The audience's reaction came rehearsed. Their curiosity, impregnated with hope, soared as if they wanted a new version of the events.

"'My last salaam on you, Sakina.' The Imam said, as he geared up to close this tragic chapter of history. Sakina pleaded with her father not to go, 'can we go to Madina?'. When the Imam mounted his horse, it wouldn't move. Then he saw his daughter standing in front of the horse, 'Please don't take away my father!' Sakina was telling him. The Imam jumped down the horse and hugged his daughter again, 'Why are you here, my moon? I said goodbye to you.'"

The voice of the speaker had broken by then too. "Akhri salaam. The last goodbye."

"Ya Hussain, Ya Hussain." The cries had now merged with the sound of thumping chests.

"'Baba, can I sleep in your arms again?' said the beloved daughter, who would always sleep on his father's chest. The Imam laid down for a few minutes, then called his sister, 'Zainab, I have to leave now. Take good care of my Sakina."

"Ya Hussain, Ya Hussain."

"The horse came back alone. Karbala went dark. Sakina waited for her father, but the enemies burnt their tents. Her dress caught fire, and she ran into the desert, asking people for directions to Najaf. 'My grandfather Ali is buried in Najaf. He helps anyone who is in need of help. I'll ask him to help us.'"

"Ya Ali, Ya Hussain."

"Oh, the cursed land of Karbala. Why didn't you shake when the daughter of the Imam was left deserted in the wilderness? The Imam used to say that a house without Sakina is not a house worth living in, and you rendered the same child homeless."

Mehar flicked a tear from the corner of her eye. Not much had changed in these fourteen hundred years.

"When the tents of the Prophet's family were attacked, the

women realised Sakina was missing. Bibi Zainab went out into the desert to find her, 'Where are you, Sakina, my child?'. And there she found her, resting her head on the chest of her dead father, sobbing. 'Baba, come back. It's dark here. They have looted our homes. They have burnt our tents. They snatched the earrings off my ears. They are bleeding now. Babaaa!"

"Ya Hussain, Ya Hussain."

Mehar went inside her room, and clicked the doors shut. This year, for a change, she would mourn in solitude.

* * *

The next day, Mehar slept till late noon. She got up and took some time to readjust herself to the changed location. Sometimes, living the reality is still the easier part than accepting it. The space in the room had shrunken owing to Shama's luggage; only one linear way afforded the possibility of one person to enter the door and leave outside to the balcony. While going towards her bathroom on the terrace, disconnected from the room, she was relieved to see that her poetry books had not been done away with, unlike most of her belongings. They still occupied a sad corner of the room, gathering dust and the angst of not being opened for years. After cleaning herself up, Mehar went down to the second floor to pick up something to prepare her meal with. She returned to her room and readied the stove that occupied the farthest corner of her room, which also doubled up as her source of heat in the winter months. She turned the vegetables in the pan and put in some oil. It would be rare for her to meet her brother and sister-in-law, with the former going to his general store early in the morning and returning late, and the sister-in-law usually at some neighbour's place or busy watching television. Mehar had started giving tuition to the kids around, basic English and Mathematics. Undoubtedly, the parents would have wanted a more socially acceptable option, but the rates Mehar offered had forced them to give a concession to their uprightness. Mehar looked outside; the light was fading. It was the pleasant weather between winter and summer, that came only for a short while in Lahore. She put the cooked vegetables on a plate and came out onto the verandah to eat; it was also pleasant without a pedestal fan.

Just then, Mehar heard the voices coming from downstairs. Her brother shouting at his wife, then the shouts became harder and temporarily ended in the sound of a hand slapping against a face. The break was only for a while, and then sounds of things being thrown around disturbed the air. Both abused in Punjabi, and Mehar was sure the neighbours were off to some entertainment, some of whom had already neared the windows of their houses to get a better version of the proceedings. Mehar did not react. She kept on eating. This reminded her of her own life a few months ago, but it didn't traumatise her. She was a product of Old Lahore; sometimes, she derided herself for her strength. Who are those people who just collapse when inconvenience hits them and never get up?

Lucky bastards.

The sounds continued. She felt pity for her sister-in-law for a moment, but was sure she had learnt enough to defend herself. And if the spouses had to show their scars in a court of law to prove who the abuser was, it would be a very tough competition. When the neighbourhood women came to Shama and abused her husband in his absence, Shama would shake away their concerns with a simple, "Beats me, but loves me as well."

When the sounds did not die for another fifteen minutes, a reel began playing in Mehar's mind. Money was scarce in her husband's house, and all that he had was spent on heroin and local booze, and then he beat Mehar to a pulp. Not that it was the only time he beat her, but the blows got particularly brawny when he was stressed. The good thing was Ahmad was often away from the house, at times for months. No one asked him where he was. He was immune to interrogation.

Mehar spent most of the time in the house with Ahmad's mother, who was a kind woman. She would come to console Mehar and tell her that all women in our society go through the same. Her husband also used to beat her, but he came around. That is what the test of being a good woman was all about. Mehar took this advice without a comment. But her mother-in-law was also a sly woman; she had learned the tricks of mastering her existence in the patriarchal setup of their home. On every mistake that Mehar made (waking up late, putting extra salt in the chicken, burning bread, forgetting to change the covers), she would take the charge sheet to her son, Mehar's husband.

"All I wanted was a good, pious woman for my son. And what I got is this good-for-nothing queen." Her mother-in-law's tears were always waiting for a subtle cue to come out.

And Mehar's test of being a good woman started again.

It was taken every night.

She passed it daily.

She wouldn't scream.

* * *

One day, about three years ago, Bina had just finished intubating a patient when she saw her phone flashing with Mehar's name. This was strange, and probably urgent as well. Contact between the two friends had dwindled since Mehar's marriage, as her husband did not allow her to use a phone. They were rare instances when Mehar could sneak her phone out from the large trunk, clandestinely arrange for it to be charged, and call someone.

"I am coming to meet you, Bina. Where are you?"

"Hospital, Mehru. Is everything alright?"

Bina was just about to be done with a 24-hour medical emergency as a house officer. She could kill to get some sleep right then, but if there was an exception she could make, it could have only been for Mehar.

"Poor Mehar," she thought.

Mehar told her mother-in-law she was leaving. She had already sought permission to go to a lady health worker regarding conception issues. It had been years since their marriage, and nothing was happening. True, it could partly be explained by Ahmad's routine absence, but there had to be more reason to it.

"What will people say about your son?"

"Don't bark. The problem must be with you."

"That is why I want to go get myself checked. If I have a problem, your son shouldn't waste time on me and bring a second wife. But in the meanwhile, imagine people doubting your son's manhood for all the fault that's mine."

It did not take much to convince a society consumed with making babies and masculinity about the necessity of all the cautionary measures that ought to be taken for maintaining honour. A son's manhood should never be up for debate.

Mehar left the house, and walked for about a kilometre before she reached the bus station. She bought a pass and sat on the first seat that caught her eye on entering the red coloured bus. She hid her face with a veil that day, fingers constantly fidgeting.

* * *

Bina went to the hospital cafeteria, where she had asked Mehar to meet her, bought some fries and a can of coke, and occupied an empty table near the counter. She tried to evade the prying eyes of her colleagues, as her capacity for social interaction was overwhelmed by fatigue.

She saw Dr. Faheem pass by, whose cheating was recently caught red-handed by his second wife; the gossip was that she caught him with a woman inside her own bedroom and abandoned both to the street in their birthday suits. Then came Dr. Mohsin, a well-meaning fellow who would subtly lecture Bina on religion and indulge in proselytising very benignly. Dr Saba came with her high-heels that announced her arrival at least two minutes in advance. She was joined by Dr. Mahvish who was clearly in a vitriolic mood against her supervising consultant. No one noticed Bina, she kept her head drooped, and dozed off after a while.

When Mehar nudged her after a brief interlude, Bina noticed that her face had lost all expression. She came back to her senses, observed Mehar's black burqa and hugged her. Bina saw a cut on Mehar's upper lip, but tried to ignore it. Mehar hugged back, though she kept her hands to herself.

"Mehru, it's so good to see you. What do I order for you?"

"Nothing, I don't have time. Bina, I have to tell you something," Mehar's tone was devoid of any hint of emotion.

"Is there a problem, Mehru? Please tell me."

"I am pregnant."

"Well…" Bina did not know how to react. "Congratulations?"

"Bina!"

"Yes?"

"I want an abortion."

"What?" Bina was running out of reactions that day.

"I don't have much time. No one else knows about it. I want it gone. Don't worry about the pain. I am used to it. Will deal with it just fine. Just make it quick. Please?"

"But Mehar, why?"

"I don't know who the father is."

Chapter Six

AFTER DEDICATED contemplation and a few frenzied nights over the issue, Bina decided to do something which she thought was unbecoming of her. She prized herself on being emotionally sound, that she would not give in to desire and vulnerability. But who was she fooling? When even the deities were helpless in the face of avarice and seduction, assuming that a mortal's resistance mechanism would not fail is expecting too much of a weak being. Besides, forgiving is an act of liberation. She wanted to make amends not only for him but also for herself as well - especially for herself. She had decided she was done with this entanglement that had to be addressed someday. Liberation doesn't come easy.

She unblocked Feroze's number and texted him. She was convinced she was texting the unsullied version of Feroze, who she fondly remembered, not the person he had become in all these years and as the world knew him now. The Feroze of her childhood, who she had cried and laughed with, who she had bruised her knees with, who she had caught tadpoles and earthworms with, who she had promised to spend her life with.

Kids are so stupid.

But they had made those promises at a time when they did not know what exactly spending one's life with someone entailed. For, in other ways, they were spending their lives with each other anyway. Their presence in each other's lives was profoundly marked by their absence.

"You can do this, Bina," she said to herself as she unlocked her phone to open WhatsApp and searched for Feroze Malik.

8:02 pm: Feroze, hi! I hope you're well. I just wasn't feeling myself on the phone that day. I know it was rude of me. Anyhow, how is everything? How is aunty coping up?

8:04 pm: Binaa, heyyy, where did you go? Not good, yaar! You haven't told me anything about yourself. I have been pretty busy these past couple of years, but now is a good time to make up for lost time.

Make up for lost time.

What is surmountable and what is not?

8:29: Yeah, Feroze. I shifted to Islamabad after completing my house job. I am getting trained here.

8:31: That's so good to hear, Bina! I always knew you would do great things. How often do you come to Sukkur? It's been ages since I went to Islamabad. We have so much to talk about.

8:40: Rarely, you know, after that happened. Sometimes, I think the place is no longer a good reminder to me. Though I cannot tell you how much I miss my Sindhu and my date trees. Those excruciating summer nights which would never end. And we did not have any ACs back then."

8:40: Haha yeah.

8:41: Hey Bina, If you cannot come here, let's plan something in Lahore. It's been so long since I met you guys. How often do you visit Lahore? Just give me a date, and I'll be there. Is Aariz currently in Pakistan? I saw his tweet. Need to see him as well. I haven't talked to him for a very long time.

Suddenly, Bina half regretted texting Feroze.

She had brought it upon herself.

She did not seek liberation. She only liked the idea of it.

Cannot do. Cannot not do.

8:59: Yes, Feroze. I'll also ask Aariz, and we'll decide on a date.

* * *

When Bina was texting Feroze, Mehar was seated on the rooftop of a three-storied house two lanes from her home. The buildings in the area were peculiar. Since the space on the ground had shrunk, people had gone vertical; the buildings now escalated from the ground into incomprehensible structures. One house merged into another, not strictly knowing which walls they shared; the rooftops were all connected; and different levels of the buildings with their unique architecture and bizarre motifs gave the place a distinct, tasteless character that many deemed artistic. On the lanes, nothing bigger than a motorcycle could pass. People would rub into each other as the traffic flow in an artery increased. This was welcome for perverts, and every now and then, a woman would slap a man for the misadventures his hands might have had.

Mehar was seated in Nashmia's house, her childhood friend who had always come to her rescue. Nashmia's family had been quite kind towards Mehar since her return to the Old City, unlike most other families. They hadn't given her disapproving looks or asked mean questions, but had continued to act regularly. This household had always been a welcome respite for Mehar from the throes of her own. Nashmia was combative and always a source of entertainment; Mehar had accepted her offer without as much as a second thought.

"What really happened, Mehar?" she asked after taking Mehar into her room before they joined the family on the rooftop.

Mehar told her.

One day, which was as fine as Mehar's other days in that house, Ahmad had returned from what he called finding work, and shouted Mehar's name. Twice. Mehar came out from the kitchen, brushing her flour-dappled hands on her apron, her mother-in-law by her side.

"Get out of my house. I divorce you."

Mehar could not understand what had transpired.

Did he know?

She stood silent. Her mother-in-law bounced her gaze from her son to her daughter-in-law, without saying a word.

"Can't you hear me? Get out of this house. I have divorced you." He flashed some papers before her; they fell to the floor.

It was pretty eventless. Mehar went to her room, threw some of her belongings in the trunk she had brought from her house, and left.

Just like that.

If Mehar's other in-laws experienced any sense of remorse for what Ahmad had done, they never expressed it.

That is how it all ended.

Age of Mehar and Ahmad's marriage: Seven years.

Age of estrangement: Seven minutes.

* * *

The end of something.

The beginning of another?

* * *

Nashmia listened to Mehar's story, and responded, *"Kutta.* He looked like a rapist anyway. It's good you're out of that hell."

Mehar accepted this token of sympathy from Nashmia. She put her hand on Nashmia's, which was still shaking with the force of the abuses she was offering Ahmad. "The blithering idiot, the forsaken pimp."

Mehar agreed with Nashmia with a soft 'hmmm'. Clearly, her agency in this conversation was limited. But Nashmia suddenly proceeded to a sensitive topic, "Mehar, why did your father do it to you?"

Mehar was caught by surprise. She had never really bothered to work out the intricacies of her father's behaviour; she had been so consumed living it that she could never afford to have a distant, academic discourse on it. She looked at Nashmia and understood that this was a genuine question from her perspective. Some daughters do have doting fathers, some daughters don't, and stuff like that.

Was Mehar the exception, or Nashmia?

Who can say?

Nashmia understood she shouldn't have broached this topic, so she immediately changed the subject.

"Tell me, Mehru, does that Sikh ghost still haunt your house? Remember how scared we were as children? The creaking of the furniture, the sound of things falling off, I'd be shit horrified to be in your home!"

Mehar laughed, "There was no ghost, Nashmia."

My house never needed ghosts to haunt it.

"Hmm, there better not have been. There's not a person in the world I'm afraid of, but ghosts, yaar, those things scare me."

When they finally joined Nashmia's family members on the rooftop, everyone embraced Mehar.

They started telling Mehar exciting stories about what was happening around them, in the houses that adjoined theirs and the lanes that ran below. Mehar listened to all without paying much attention. During a ruckus caused by a leaking water pipe that ran downwards from the roof, Mehar stood up and went towards the roof's edge.

"Don't jump, Mehru," Nashmia shouted.

Mehar smiled. She couldn't even if she wanted to. She was cursed to brave everything. A child of Old Lahore. A child of nothing, with nothing to lose.

Not even her own life.

She looked around. Multicoloured houses in faded paint bolstered shiny blue plastic water tanks as far as the eyes could see. Some walls of the swampy houses were denuded of the plaster, their bricks came out upon each other from various angles. On others, an intricate jharokha or traditional motif would belie the otherwise sorry condition of things, and present an appeal of lost glory. Many shapes could be drawn from the vision of the Old City there: figures that defied the rules of geometry, that became borderless the more you observed them. Suddenly, there was a call for the Isha prayer. It was deafening, as Nashmia's house was in a lane just behind the Wazir Khan mosque. Mehar went to the other end of the rooftop to see the mosque. The newly installed floodlights duly lighted up its meticulous design and colourful frescoes.

She looked at it for quite some while.

The mosque's story was something Mehar had often told her friends. She was once considered an expert on old buildings, and was obsessed with them. The mosque was made by one Ilam ud Din Ansari, who had migrated to Lahore some five hundred years ago. His pilgrimage to the city served him well. He became a physician in Mughal Emperor Shah Jahan's court, and was made a noble and given the title of Wazir Khan over the years. He had remained the governor of Agra before being appointed as Lahore's.

Today, every visitor to the Old City comes inside its gates repeating the name: Wazir Khan.

Mehar suddenly felt a disdain for the monument and what it represented. So many people squandered their entire lives treading on a wire of thorns, but only some were rewarded. Who will remember the struggles of all the others? For every Wazir Khan remembered, there were a hundred other Wazir Khans, and a thousand other Mehars forgotten by history; the memory of time being a finite resource.

The *azaan* had ended. The water pipe had been fixed. Mehar returned to where the chairs were placed in the centre of the rooftop, a fire burning inside her. She spotted a gecko on her way back, lifelessly clinging to the floor of the roof. Its body had been punctured owing to a fall on the running pedestal fan, the miscalculated jump had had it mutilated by the fan's running blades and thrown off onto the floor.

Mehar looked at the despicable state of the gecko for a while and then squished it under her foot.

Chapter Seven

IT HAD been a few days after Aariz's return to Lahore, and he was still grappling with how fast the city had progressed in the years he wasn't here. The shopping malls in Lahore now competed with those of Europe, fine dining had taken on a full form in the city, different "indie" activities were now a regular in the city's schedules of activities. His own schedule had remained busy; he had to meet a lot of his and his father's friends; and all of them fed him with the gratuitous details of unnecessary things that people had an infatuation with. More pressingly, he had to interview freelancers for his consultancy work. Whenever he got the time, he would roam around the city, only to find versions of himself that awaited him. And he would look at them, consoling but not embracing them, and move on.

The fact that Zainab, Khaala's daughter, was such a prying little devil was cumbersome for Aariz. She could be found sneaking around everywhere; in that cupboard, in that drawer, under this table; something that bothered Aariz and he chastised her for. Zainab, for her part, was finding dollars (to look at, not steal), but all she ever found unattended were notes with a man wearing an Arabic headgear.

Aariz took his time cleaning the mess in his apartment. He postponed the activity of perusing items and discarding them, as it would be quite toilsome. But when he finally sat down one evening to clear the clutter from the drawers of his room's wardrobe, he discovered a diary with Mickey Mouse on its cover. He attended to it immediately, and clutched it as he sat on the edge of his bed. This diary was a young Aariz's biggest treasure; it was the only part of his life where access to Old Papa was also forbidden. Aariz smiled at the recollection.

He opened the diary, and read the title, written in his desperate cursive, "The Secrets of Cosmos, Aariz Ali".

It was his way of deciphering the complexities that Old Papa had thrown at him. Every page of the diary had one question, and about three-fourths of the pages were consumed. As Aariz shuffled the pages, the questions met him.

"Does a tree grow inside you if you eat a seed?"

"Can a big snake eat a crocodile?"

"What is the age of my ceiling fan?"

"Does my mama miss me?"

"Does someone watch me when I sleep?"

"In which book is my destiny written?"

"What is the age of God?"

"Why was the world black and white in old times?"

Aariz smiled with a peculiar warmth that you only reserve for a memory of yourself. He slipped directly to the last entry of the diary, and the question was something that had remained unanswered all along.

"How did Old Papa die?"

* * *

The most important question of all: how did Old Papa die?

That is a question for historians to answer.

Or doctors.

But in Aariz's mind, the death played out in a slow, animated sequence, much like a whimper instead of a blast. He was woken up by the wails of his mother, first mistaking them to be a dream before realising that he had already crossed the line between dream and reality. He came out of his room into the lounge, and that is where mama was - crying. Aariz saw the person standing with her. He had a rubber tube around his neck and headphones attached to it. He had seen doctors wearing those in movies as well. Aariz was always bemused by one thing, why did the doctors always have headphones in their ears while people around them were dying? Clearly, it seemed like an insensitive thing to do, to listen to music while people shrieked around you.

Maybe, it was their escape?

Maybe, they also heard voices they wanted to mute?

And where was Old Papa anyway?

Mama was shifting between crying and proclaiming incessantly, "But he was perfectly fine. He was healthy; he exercised. He had no issues at all. He got sick a month ago, and we took all the tests. Everything was normal..."

The doctor listened patiently, on occasions like these, every doctor is usually in a fix to decide how much to put on medical science, and how much on the design of the cosmos.

"He had a cardiac arrest, Mrs. Ali. His heart just stopped beating. It can be due to a number of reasons."

"But there was no reason here. His heart was perfectly fine..."

The doctor looked at his feet.

What was there to say?

Only that the woman before him was now a widow. Only that the child that stood at the corner of the room, scared, was now an orphan.

"I am really sorry to tell you that your husband is no more. I wish there was something I could do."

Mama bowed out to the floor, snivelling. The doctor hung around her, confused whether or not to put a hand around her shoulder.

Aariz tiptoed to his parents' room. Was Old Papa pulling off a practical joke? Only Aariz would be able to tell.

There he was. Old Papa. Stunning as ever, but whiter than usual. Lying still on the bed, with his eyes closed. He was wearing what he usually wore to bed, trousers with a vest. He could just be sleeping.

Aariz neared his father's body and kissed him on the cheek. The cold-bodied Old Papa didn't kiss him back. It was all that was needed to tell Aariz that Old Papa was no more. Still, he pushed. He laughed and tickled him, but to no response. That is when Aariz's laughter disappeared into the big black hole in the cosmos where his father's heart beat had gone to. He was guzzled by impending fear; the grief came later.

"His heart just stopped beating."

Aariz was hit by how it would have happened. It was like it happens in movies. Old Papa's heart was previously beating continuously, to a tune that would imitate a watch.

Tick, tick, tick...

It was pumping blood to all the parts of his body, giving them food. To his lips that smiled at Aariz. To his arms that held Aariz. To his face that he immersed in Aariz's belly. To his shoulders that carried Aariz. To his fingers that fed Aariz. And then, it stopped beating, like a watch running out of batteries.

Just like that.

And in a nano-second, Old Papa shifted from the place of the living to the place of the dead.

Would Old Papa have survived had Aariz changed his heart's batteries on time?

Who can say?

* * *

"Historically, the Japanese have been killing themselves for a greater cause. They think that if a life is not worth living, it's better to redirect those sources somewhere else," Aariz commented.

Dr. Nadeem, the psychiatrist, interjected, "No, Aariz, I am the doctor here. Please don't feed me half baked theories ripped off Durkheim. This is not how it functions."

"I am just telling you there are various views on it. Why can't you understand I am not depressed?"

"You casually talk about death and the end of life and tell me you're not depressed?"

"Death is just a continuum, like time. Our idea of death is narrowed by our limited capacity to think. We worry about the great unknown that lies after it. "

"So Aariz, what secrets have you decoded about life?"

"That there are no secrets to decode."

"Have you been using any drugs?"

"Nothing that has helped me."

"What help do you need, exactly? I'm giving you medication that I gave last time and you did not use. "

"Those do not help."

"You cannot tell me that without using them."

"I did."

"Aariz, look, you know your father was such a dear friend of mine. You belong to such a good family. Please tell me the problem."

"Do problems also decide what sort of family they want to fall upon?"

"You are talking like a ten-year old," Uncle Nadeem spat.

"Uncle Nadeem, I have told you there is no problem like you think there is. Let's just agree that I am made differently. "

"I will not contest that. But mental illness is nothing that can hamper you from anything. So many great people in history were depressed, to the point of being suicidal, but they achieved great things - not despite their illness but because of it. Take Abraham Lincoln, or Oscar Wilde."

Aariz scoffed, "I am not here to glorify mental illness, uncle. I am just saying that I feel differently, and it's not easy to explain how."

"Do you surround yourself with good people?"

"Yes, uncle. I have a number of friends, I work well, I am

successful; there's nothing that you can ascribe my state to. "

"Did something happen in your life that changed you?"

"If something did, it would only have enhanced how I naturally am."

"Sadness can be a natural state. The Buddha also said everything is inherently sad."

Aariz controlled himself from contesting the widespread misunderstandings that people had normalised. It was similar to the cars he had recently seen in Lahore with Che Guevera plastered on their rear windows; people displayed the man with little understanding of what he stood for and were completely unaware of his beliefs that they might find disagreeable otherwise. But he chose to just play along, "And for him, the panacea is to get detached from everything. I already am. Now what?"

"What do you mean, you're detached?" I have heard you are very kind towards your peers. "

"Uncle, everything in life is performative. Everything. It's easy to put up a show of something while not being infused by it. Some things you do because you have to. I am not un-empathetic only because I can not naturally feel empathy. Not to blow my own trumpet, but I have an IQ higher than the average. I know what is proper and what is not."

"So you function well in your life?"

"Apparently, perfectly."

"Is apparently the functional word here?"

"It is."

"Do you think things would change if something changed in your life?"

"Uncle, look, I don't know how to explain it because I know it sounds strange. I don't feel what people are supposed to feel. I have everything in my life. There's nothing I want to change, but having everything has just made it clear to me that there's nothing in it for me. This is all consistent drudgery, nothing else. I appreciate everything, I am grateful for all there is, but nothing makes any sense to me. It's not because my mind is not functioning, but probably because it's functioning too much. "

"Medication may help you make sense of things."

"Medication will make it worse if it tries to do that. The more you try to locate sense, the more you understand it's not there. If you could make my mind numb and take away from me the power to see things as they are, that would be great. Otherwise it's a lost cause. "

"We can see the treatment options, Aariz."

"Doctor, my treatment is my disease."

* * *

Aariz left Uncle Nadeem's clinic. Coming here had been a ritual since the day New Papa had decided Aariz wasn't well and should be seeing a shrink. Mama said she knew one of Old Papa's friends, so Aariz landed here. And through all these years, Aariz had been saying the same things. Over and over again. In different words and with different expressions - but to no avail. He knew the visits were a scam, but they had become one of those habits that aren't easy to part with. Besides, Aariz could say whatever he wanted to, and not a lot of places allowed him that liberty.

Because what was there to say?

How do you explain to someone that you're wary of life not because you've been defeated by it, but because you've triumphed over it; and that what people believe to be the pinnacle of existence is just another hoax that all men and women are chasing? The tried-and-tested formula for happiness is to make people want something. It is for want that people pursue a job, a partner in bed, money, and power. The greatest trick ever played on humans: keep them busy till they die.

Make them want something, always.

Want is a strange thing.

But what if you don't want anything? What if you see that all this game of pawns and rooks is checkmate for you anyway?

But where did it start?

A long, long time ago.

* * *

God created Adam and Eve, the epitome of His creation, and kept them in the heavens with him.

"I will make upon the Earth a successive authority." He announced it prior to the creation of man. But the angels were apprehensive. "Will you place on it one who corrupts it and sheds blood?" they inquired.

God replied, "I know what you don't know."

Free from worries and answers and also endowed with the gift of knowledge, Adam and Eve lived a happy life in the heavens, albeit no one could really judge its purpose then. God bestowed all the bounties on them, instructing Adam to live in paradise with his wife and eat whatever he pleased.

But He also prohibited them from eating from one tree. The test in a human's life was set up concurrently with life itself.

But Adam and Eve were humans, and as their descendants would testify for thousands of years, they made mistakes that they later regretted. They were lured by Satan and ate the forbidden fruit. Their nakedness was at once apparent to them, and they started covering themselves up with the leaves of the paradise.

"Did I not forbid you from that tree and warn you that Satan is a clear enemy to you?" God asked them.

He sent Adam and Eve to the Earth from the heavens. They cried, separated and lost. God had transformed them into beings that were mortal, who had to work and who could have and raise children. They asked for forgiveness, which they were granted, but all of their progeny would have to live through the same experience - replete with temptations and regrets - for all the times to come.

Time is a continuum.

The story of the first and the last man on Earth will be the same.
The age of creation: uncountable.
The age of frustration: uncountable.

** * **

And where does it end?
Who can say?
But what is the secret?
It is to become everything.

Chapter Eight

IN THE weeks after his father's *chehlum,* Feroze often found himself wandering through uncharted territory. His intent of becoming a member of the provincial assembly was still unrealised; the party had refused to give him a ticket as it viewed him as too callow to take on the charge - much to Hashmatullah's acrimony. Feroze wasn't sure if he wanted the position anymore since the only person vying for that achievement was gone.

Feroze came out of the lounge, rested, and took a seat at the mouth of the lawns bounded by date trees swirling in the air, the dying outline of many of which was exposed to him. He was relieved to receive Bina's texts and could not wait to meet her.

And Aariz.

Approaching Bina had somewhat been more manageable; they had been so close that decorum didn't always have to feature in the equation always, or so he thought. But he had refrained from approaching Aariz. The emotion had prevented him from doing so, and he had only realised recently what that emotion had been, all along, shame.

He was puzzled at how readily he had let some people flee his life. More so because it was the people his life had revolved around greatly. Where had the clarity gone?

"The clarity had gone up in the smoke of a dead father's cigar," the Gorgon smirked.

Feroze looked for a while, thoughtless, in the expanse that lay before him and spread out into the great cosmos.

He had paused all his political activities for the time being, even while his late father's advisors considered this a folly of the most significant degree. This was his time to take over, forcefully, the vacuum left by his father. To impress upon the people who always need a saviour - sometimes in the form of a saint, sometimes a leader - that only a man was dead, the dynasty wasn't. He wasn't really interested in politics ever, anyway. Even if he had gotten an opportunity to say this to his father, he had rarely seized it. You don't turn your back on what is, by default, yours. Besides, what would his father have said? He'd be disgruntled, telling Feroze that his only son had failed him.

A firefly buzzed around him; he caught it by an intricate movement of his arm; a commentator would say he was copying Wasim Akram. Feroze let the fly go after a while. It buzzed around for another half a minute, and left through a break in the air, to never return.

Like his father.

And his grandfather.

Feroze had few memories of his grandfather, and he could not tell if they were particularly pleasant. He was a busy man, always cocooned by flocks of people and on the run against time. But he was greatly esteemed by those around him, or at least that is what they said. He achieved so much, starting with so little; everyone would tell Feroze. As a child, he learned to look up to him, first the person, and after his death, the memory. Feroze looked at the cover of the diary he held in his left hand, which he hadn't touched since the day he had embezzled it from his father's library. The leather had been thwarted in places, the buckle that bound it cut in half. Feroze opened it. His grandfather's immaculate handwriting greeted him. He thumbed through the pages for a while. He started reading the first entry but did not know when he was taken over by sleep, but by then, the pages had started talking.

* * *

"Time is a continuum. It seems only yesterday when we had to come to Hoshiarpur from Haryana, for the basic reason that all human migrations take place. I was a kid then - barely four or five - and cannot recollect much. My father used to tell me this wasn't the only time we had to move; our family went to Haryana from Punjab two generations preceding his, as my great grandfather got a job in one of the firms set up by the white people there after the failed War of Independence in 1857. So coming to Hoshiarpur wasn't as much of a migration as it was a homecoming. But history kept on repeating itself. The land of India kept throwing us around, chucking us from one place to another. And sixty years later, after I had set up a life in Hoshiarpur - complete with all the essentials that a man is expected to have - we had to migrate again. It's probably the oldest human activity: migrating. Sometimes willingly, sometimes reluctantly; sometimes from the skies to the land, sometimes from the desert to an oasis.

India was up in hot smoke. The British had decided to leave, not due to the freedom movements of the locals as much as their impending bankruptcy owing to the Second World War. I went to the war, fought in the Battle at Dunkirk, and came back unharmed, except for a shrapnel that had entered my leg, giving me a limp for a lifetime. Upon returning, I saw a different India from the one that I had left. The social structures had all given way, exposing the rotten core of Indian society. But what was really rotten was the August of 1947, and what came around it.

India was going to be independent; there was no doubt about it. Now, it was something people said openly in the streets, not only in enclosed quarters of white backgrounds. The goras had started leaving, first in silence, then openly. But the question in India wasn't about the *goras'* leaving, but what they would leave behind. What will be the India they were going to leave behind for the locals?

The Mahatma was clear it had to be one country, which was arguable given that India had always been a conglomeration of states. To solve this, the goras gave the option of deciding their destiny over to the 593 states themselves. But another man had risen up to prominence in India, Mr. Jinnah. He, and his Muslim League, avowed to have another country carved out of India as well: Pakistan. I was never a fan of his political ideology, the idea of Pakistan sounded like a fiasco to so many of us, but nevertheless, one could not doubt the man's stature. I like intelligent and efficient people; Jinnah was the quintessential poster boy of these traits. Pakistan was mapped to be composed of the Muslim majority areas of NWFP, Sindh, Balochistan, Kashmir, Punjab, and Bengal. We were to be a part of Pakistan. With no effort on our part, all we had to do was to wake up one morning and accept that we were in a different country already, without having to migrate. In a new country, opportunities are unlimited. We were relaxed.

But everything changed in the June of that dastardly year. As temperatures soared in India, they also brought along the Radcliffe Award, and then everything fell over. Hoshiarpur, which was to be a part of Pakistan, was given to India. Lines were drawn across Punjab and Bengal. India would later annex Junagarh and Hyderabad as well. My initial reaction to hearing the news might have been a passing sense of grief, as I had already worked upon the ways to fit in the infant structure of a crumbling new state, but staying in India was, for all practical purposes, the saner prospect that came with stability. Basically, nothing was to change for us.

But there was a concern: the riots; they were inhumanly tragic. The news of the carnage started doing the rounds as early as June, but our area kept enjoying the lull before the storm, desperately in denial. Every day, we heard of villages of Muslims torched to a crisp in the Punjab that was potentially India, and every day hordes of Sikhs and Hindus came running all the way from the Punjab that was to be Pakistan. The survivors told fiercely brutal stories about what they had seen, and Ravi turning red due to the colour of blood was the least of them. And one day, we became the victims. Just like that, without a warning or premonition. There was some news doing the rounds that all the Muslim houses in the village had been clandestinely marked a day before, but I couldn't find anything testifying to such sensationalism. Besides, I was of the view that the rich standing of my family would somehow protect me from the riots. I was a fool to believe that money could withstand a planned massacre. Money isn't always the saviour, even if it mostly is.

That night, a mob broke into our village in the dark of night. Ours was a big village, and our house was relatively protected owing to its peripheral location. We could see the fire in the farther ends of the village; the smoke carried the screams of the women and children to us. Those are the sounds that, even after all these years, I cannot forget. They wake me up at night, and the smoke chokes my nostrils still. It sounded like a sacrificial ritual, which the British had banned in India only to facilitate it later.

Only my wife and two children were in the house at that time with me, with my only brother already working in Karachi as an Indian Civil Servant. Then there were the servants, and I told them to look after the house. I got my family out. Shakooran was scared and grabbed the little Shahida in her arms, but Hashmat was adamant. He cried, saying he would take his books with him, that his exams were approaching. He was always a moody child and took more readily to books than people. I dragged him along, and we all came out of the house, and that is where he threw a tantrum again: he sat on the ground and started crying, stomping his feet on the ground and screaming like the child he was. Shakooran decided to cajole him into leaving, but he wouldn't listen. I grabbed him by the arm and slapped him across his face. He did not say a thing after that. In fact, he has been silent in front of me since that day.

We crossed our fields and ran towards the side of Kharkan, instead of going towards Amritsar. We travelled the whole night in our tonga, and it was dawn when we reached the house of Akbar

Hotiana. Akbar was my friend and held influence over the area, yet we were careful about being discrete in our journey. Akbar kept us in his home for three days, after which he arranged for us to fly to Karachi from Delhi. My life, as I had known it, ended in a flash. You take so much to build something, and all it takes is a moment for it to end.

But it wasn't death. Just the end of one life.

It was also the beginning of another.

We landed in Karachi, where we had informed Takbeer, my brother, of our arrival. Takbeer told us that Punjab was brimming with immigrants, and it wasn't wise to go there, lest we wanted to die in a burning, overcrowded refugee camp. Karachi was a pothole of people as well, so he put us through to his friend in Sukkur in upper Sindh, a man called Vinkesh Vankwani. Takbeer had been in Karachi for so many years that he had acquaintances all over, especially in this province. Many Hindus from Sindh had also gone to India, and their properties could be claimed by us through the Evacuee Board. Takbeer would deal with the legalities of the act. As I said, there was so much that could be done in the infant state of Pakistan.

Vinkesh and I soon settled into a relationship of convenience. He was a businessman and hadn't left for India as he related more with Sindh than either India or Pakistan. Since I had also run dairy farms in Hoshiarpur, I started working with him. Vinkesh's son, Shreeshant, became Hashmat's friend; that is the most lively I have seen Hashmat since that night. I got the spare land of an escaped Hindu family; I would build on it over the years. For many years, Vinkesh and I would work together; honestly, it was more beneficial for me than for him. We expanded our business, starting with agriculture produce and culminating in import-export.

Sometime later, I realised that the political situation in Sindh was precarious; the Muslim League that had been the torchbearer of the Pakistan Movement wasn't extremely popular here, and

Sindh's nationalist parties were challenging it every day. I joined this party of Sindh - it had many intellectuals and liberals - and soon levelled up its ranks. In upper Sindh, the dialect of their language is not very different from ours. I mastered it, and it wasn't long before people would forget that I was not one of them..."

* * *

Feroze woke up, startled. He had never tried to deconstruct his father as a person. For him, he had just been an idea to aspire for. The fact that he had once cried for his books and was prone to give in to moods belied the stature that Feroze had been used to. He realised that his grandfather's diary wasn't a daily journal, but general recollections from his life, possibly from right before he died. Feroze went straight to the last entry of the diary.

"Looking back, I am glad I settled in Sindh. The place carries traditions of thousands of years. Vinkesh was right; Pakistan and India were featherlight concepts, and Sindh was eternal - right from the time of Mohenjodaro. The age of the two countries could be counted on the fingers, but the history of Sindh can be traced back to 9000 years. The saints and Sufis who lived in Sindh have emboldened this place's inclusivity and diversity. Even at this age, I am shocked by the presence of at least one shrine inside every lake in the province. It is the safest place in the country and offers the most in terms of religions and traditions. Nothing explains Sindh better than Shah Abdul Latif Bhittai and his seven queens who defied the outlandish ideas and stood up for principles: Lilan, Sohni, Noori, Marui, Moomal, Suraths, and Sassui."

Feroze closed the diary. He had heard his father say the same about Sindh all the time. He went to his room.

* * *

In the night, the pages ruffled after Feroze had slept. They had read themselves so many times over these years, and had gotten wary of what was written on them. Indeed, there had to be more to this? The pages wanted to fly some one thousand kilometers to the north of the country, and wanted a woman who was prescribing medicines to her patients in the Outpatient Department of the largest hospital in Islamabad to write her edition of the events as well. The woman would have written something like, "It's difficult to draw the line between fiction and reality. Recollection of the past is always a biased exercise. There can be obscene differences between what really happened and what one says happened. While the dancing girl of Mohenjodaro is being fought after by the two countries that are not sure how to claim their shared history, the Nooris and Maruis of Sindh are now being abducted, furthered by the political agenda of bigots. It's partly tragic, partly comic, how the oppressed become the oppressors. About a century ago, my grandfather opened his doors for a homeless man who had come staggering at our door. He helped him make a home in a place that was ours, had been ours since the existence of Sorath and Moomal. Years later, we learned that he had officially transferred half of our property in his name. We didn't say a word; we just let Jhulelaal do his thing.

And then, worse happened.

In 1992, a mosque was destroyed in Ayodhya, in another country, which we clearly had nothing to do with, but clarifications were sought from us nonetheless. It started a succession of riots in our homeland: our temples were destroyed, our homes attacked. Soon, the occupation of our lands started. As this happened, the son of the same man who had come to our door - and who was now apparently friends with my father - offered to take our property in his name so that it could be protected. It would be returned as the dust settled, he told us.

But promises are rarely kept, as Lilan and Sohni also experienced. We soon realised that this act done on the pretext of protection was a brazen occupation. And that is how another

Sassui of Sindh was left wandering in the desert, uprooted from her home."

Time is a continuum.
History repeats itself.
Where does the oppressed end and the oppressor begin?
Who can say?

Chapter Nine

THE OLD City of Lahore is a world unto itself. Its origin is disputed, but all agree it has existed since times so ancient that even historians grapple with an exact date. Some say it was founded by Luv, the son of Ram; others contend this proposition seems historically unsettling, but most agree that during the Mughal Emperor Akbar's reign, the area got some of its present form with him having shifted his capital from Fatehpur Sikri to Lahore. It is a detailed grid of lanes and houses, with the focus of the establishment being the Royal Fort. Also known as Walled City, it is a cosmos of monuments, cuisines, bazaars, traditions, sights, and sounds. It houses many havelis, mosques, and wells; some more eager to narrate what they have seen than others. Conservation has been taking place in the area for quite a while, recasting some areas of the Walled City into tourist hubs. Fancy, exotic hotels catering to locals and foreigners alike have been set up in the vicinity of the Mughal Mosque; they light up like a half-remembered fable at night.

It was the time when Basant was still not banned in Lahore, which came about as the chemical strings of kites would sharply open up so many throats every year, severing an infant's wobbly head while it clung to its mother. The Walled City romped to life during this festival: the celebration of spring. The kite owners' business would detonate, competitions would be arranged between neighbors and families, and people would throng the already crowded clearings to access the skies. Every now and then, someone's kite would be cut off. The kids would run to fetch it, and the winner would take all, inspiring a sense of reverence from all the other kids for one year. Loud music would blare from every house and strike against the tympanic membranes of all. No one would mind. Basant was their greatest cultural event.

It was also the time when fathers became men and husbands became pimps.

On a day when the Old City of Lahore was crayoned with a hundred colours, Mehar's life turned sepia.

Her *rukhsati* was a bland affair, not as much an event as a formality. She had been married to Ahmad when she was thirteen, but Ahmad had to leave the country soon afterward in search of greener pastures, and it was settled the *rukhsati* would be done only on his return. No one wants an extra mouth to feed, especially if it's unrelated. It could be said with a sense of surety that Ahmad had not really found the greener pastures he had voyaged for; his pilgrimage had gone up in vain.

It had been about eight years. During this time, Mehar had pretty much shrugged off the validity of what had transpired. The thirteen-year-old had coyly signed the wedding papers, the *nikahanama*, without any protest. How much could a mere stroke of a pen change anyway? And in these years, the seriousness of that signature had mellowed upon her. She continued her life like usual. She studied, she read poetry, she got into medical college.

But she stopped going to the monuments.

And then Ahmad returned.

On the thirteenth of April.

Haste ensued. The girl had to be sent to her house as soon as possible. Mehar had two houses now, without having either.

No one really bothered to care about her education, or her, for that matter.

That day, in the morning, Mehar went to her father and sat on the floor.

"*Abba,* please don't."

Abba stayed silent in the beginning, his expression reeking of contained vitriol. Mehar started sobbing, "I will not go with him. I want to live here. I will do whatever you say."

Abba kicked his daughter sitting at his knee.

An older man kicked a younger woman sitting at his knee.

"I am becoming a doctor, *Abba.* Please wait for that."

Abba ignored her that time and headed for the door.

For the first time in her life, consumed by terror and angst, Mehar started yelling. A monument of Old Lahore gave way and came dashing to the ground.

She screamed, and wailed, and begged. She implored him not to send her away like this, to a person she didn't know. She would just lie around a corner in the house, not registering her existence with anyone. And on completing her education, she'd leave forever. Not showing any of them her face, ever.

When the incantations failed, she shouted, gripped with the sensation of impending doom, some tactless words. She screamed what a wretched father hers had always been and was. She hollered insults at him, and cursed him for being so pathetic. That she would never forgive him. That he would never be forgiven. That she despised him, deeply and intensely, and would continue to do so till the day she dies; and wished she was not born to him.

Abba lunged at her. Clutched her by the hair and spat, "Scream like that in your husband's bed."

Fathers were men.

Mehar wept for a while relentlessly and, unconsoled, ignored her mother, who was busy pretending nothing unwonted was happening; she looked at Asad *bhai*, who did not look back. *Ama* came to her room later and told her to change into a red dress. She did without a word, came downstairs, and, looking at the floor, left that house with Ahmad. Her shimmering red lehenga the colour of blood, her red-rimmed swollen eyes the colour of death. The deceased name of Satnam Singh (in Gurmukhi script) looked down at her from atop the house's entry door as she exited it. No one remembered writing the name of another person haunted away from that house below it.

Mehar Qayyum. (In Shahmukhi script)

* * *

Mehar and Bina never got to have a proper farewell impregnated with lacrimal fluid and well wishes. They did not get to celebrate - or mourn - Mehar's last day in medical college, as it had come without warning. Mehar had had a routine day in her college, skimming through Pathology lectures and preparing a test for the next day, when she went to her house and discovered that it had been her last. She asked Asad *bhai* to get her original documents back from college, and he agreed casually, but Mehar never took a follow-up from him. But she should have realised that when her existence didn't count for much, what would pieces of paper ascertaining the same be worth? Bina learned about Mehar's ordeal some days after the latter had left the Old City and shifted to Dharampura. She had tried calling her, but it was impossible to get to Mehar. She did not have her home address.

Mehar had never given it to her.

She had never asked.

They both had known that for Mehar, home was not a place.

* * *

The first slap did not wait. It came on the wedding night.

Ahmad entered the room late, after Mehar had been duly denuded of anything she might have brought from her parents' house. Her mother-in-law had checked her purse twice to see if there was anything she had skipped and commented, dejected, "Only six thousand rupees." Then she held Mehar's face in her hands and commented, "Her eyes are big but empty, the features are very average, but *chalo*, at least she is fair."

The neighbourhood women who sat around her nodded their heads in agreement, "As fair as the moon!"

The sun became the moon. It was only the teaser of the changes Mehar had to brace herself for. And then, another woman said, as if telling a secret, "But Ahmad could have done far better."

Every man in Lahore could have always done far better.

His gait suggested an overdose of alcohol as he came inside the room. He locked the door and looked at Mehar with eyes glazed with lust moulded into abhorrence. He lit a cigarette, a cheap Capstan cigarette, and kept eyeing Mehar skeptically for a while.

Mehar doesn't remember many details from that night anymore. Probably because she does not want to remember.

Want is a strange thing.

But there are some recollections her mind doesn't assist her in forgetting.

She remembers hearing her name in a male voice, *Meharrrr,* that ended in a spit.

She remembers him telling her he was duped into marrying her, as he was told she was beautiful, but all she was, was voluptuous, testifying to the invitations she had given to other men. The comment ended with Ahmad looking at Mehar's chest scornfully.

She remembers that a hand had come towards her, falling off her hair to her powdered face, brushing against her lips, and then going away only to return quickly as a bitter slap.

She remembers a middle-aged male body slowly disrobing, first the qameez, then the shalwar, and then gnawing at the seams of her dress, slashing it.

She remembers teeth inserted into her waist, forming permanent marks on her skin.

She remembers a burning cigarette trying to enter her right breast.

She remembers something entering her, bruising her body and ripping her soul. Again and again.

She remembers whimpering like a fractured dog.

She remembers the smell of blood, sweat, spirit - and defeat.

She remembers the thud of the fall of the man beside her before he said, "Tomorrow, I will introduce you to my friends."

Husbands were pimps.

She does not remember promising herself she would never scream in life again.

Chapter Ten

WHEN BINA came home to Sukkur for the winter vacation after the first year of medical school, nothing had prepared her for the sordid surprise she was to be fed with. Bogged down with chagrin, Kamla *Bua's* monologue was fraught with hysteria, "She was born in Sharda Peeth, when we had gone for a pilgrimage there, a month before she was due. As I carried a picture of the goddess to my heart to the stairs leading us to the temple during the *yatra,* it was there that my water broke. We thought this to be Saraswati's blessing on her and named her after the *devi*. And the goddess blessed her, our Sharda is also adept in knowledge, is so wise, and has always...." Kamla *Bua's* voice trailed off as she continued. Her words couldn't perfectly portray the pain anymore.

Bina's mind had wandered elsewhere. There are things that you innately consider yourself immune to; some things are meant for others. You can read and empathise with them, but you slide past the need to prepare to deal with them. You are only supposed to live them vicariously.

What do you do when they happen to you?

* * *

In the north of the country, in a place called Kashmir, which has been in dispute for 75 years between two neighbouring countries, each willing to draw its own lines around the area, there once existed a venerated place of worship. It attracted devotees from all around, even as far as Bengal. Historians described the temple as a place of miracles. Epics from foregone eras proclaim the goddess Saraswati could herself be seen in the form of a swan here. Bilhana, the 11th-century Kashmiri poet, described the goddess as "a swan, who carries as her diadem the glittering gold washed from the sand of the Madhumati stream. Spreading lustre by her fame, brilliant like crystal, she makes even Mount Himalaya, the preceptor of Gauri, raise higher his head in pride of her existence there." Some believed that the goddess Sharda worshipped in the Sharda Peeth is a tripartite embodiment of the goddess Shakti: Sharda, Saraswati, and Vagdevi.

After 1947, Sharda Peeth declined in the number of visitors it erstwhile received. The conflict of Kashmir underscoring the issue, many pilgrims from across the border were denied permission to visit the temple as it was too close to the Line of Control.

The line.

There were three important temples in Kashmir once: Martand Sun Temple, Amarnath Temple, and the Sharda Peeth. A war over Kashmir between Pakistan and India divided them.

Our Kashmir.

Your Kashmir.

Sharda belongs here.

Amarnath belongs there.

The division was a cumbersome process, with the geographical aspect being the most tractable of the lot. Since nothing among memories, pain, or history could be divided, both the countries staggered with the remnants that occupied them.

But the temples still found a place of belonging. For many people in these two countries, belonging was hard to come by.

The great historian Al-Biruni recorded in his writings that Sharda was an esteemed shrine and housed a wooden image of Sharda Devi. Visitors today will find that the wooden image of

Sharda is long gone from the temple.

And Kamla *Bua* told Bina that day that their Sharda was gone.

* * *

After Shreeshanth had lost all he had to Hashmatullah, he reticently accepted the reality of his existence in the shadow of the crescent moon. He felt betrayed by his friend, but he never gave words to his feelings, for he knew that his eternal Sindh had become a victim of the partial amnesia of time, and the rules of the game of survival had changed in his homeland. But if turning into an oppressor from the oppressed is one thin line, Hashmatullah decided to balance the act by not jumping the line anymore. Shreeshanth continued to live in the house that was now Hashmat's property, like his father had continued to live in the Sindh that had become Pakistan. The two men stopped talking to each other, despite remaining partners in the mutual chunk of business. The financial dynamics of Shreeshanth's family stayed, for the most part, unperturbed. He was able to give his children a decent education, and the days of the family were spent with a certain comfort. But he homed a fear inside, as all of this settlement depended upon the whims of Hashmatullah, with the ownership bequeathed to him. Shreeshanth eventually started saving arduously to direct his resources to score a property in the city of Karachi. Hashmatullah could have chosen to do worse, but he looked the other way, while Shree's most pressing concern remained the friendship that had already gotten strong between his daughter and the son of his ex-friend.

Shree never sought any revenge, primarily because he couldn't - Hashmatullah's political stature had risen to such prominence that it would be ludicrous to fight him. But also because his idea of justice was to extend it to those who lived in its denial, something he inculcated in his younger daughter, Bina.

1992 was the year when it all happened. As a group of people on the other side of the line brought down an old mosque, ambivalent about tackling the undivided history that mocked them, the repercussions travelled across the border. In the wake of the attacks on Hindus in Pakistan, Hashmatullah played his cards slyly to absolve Shree of his property. And in a succession of attacks on temples in Pakistan, Shree's distant cousin, Gopal, was killed in a place called either Umerkot or *Amarkot*, depending on where you start in history. He left behind a widow, heavily pregnant with a second child.

The woman was called Kamla, and Shree brought her to his home in Sukkur. Their small family increased by two members, then three, as Kamla delivered another daughter, Rashmi, months later. Kamla *Bua* would help around the chores of the house, asking for nothing but shelter in return. Bina immediately took a liking to Sharda, an infant, who became the younger sister Bina never had. After Feroze, it was Sharda that fuelled Bina's life. Bina owned Sharda, with the irritating bossiness and the unyielding support only an elder sister can extend.

After Kamla *Bua* had narrated to Bina the ordeal as it had happened, Bina had been numb for a while. Then she knew what she had to do, even if a year had passed since their last conversation. But one year was surmountable, Bina thought.

She dialled Feroze's number.

* * *

"Feroze!"

"Bina, how are you?"

She still made the hair on his arms rise.

Their conversations had become infrequent over the years, not for any concrete reason, but the usual divergence that life leads you to. Every time they talked, Bina thought they lost another iota of the effortless candor they were previously capable of. Even when both of them had lived in Sukkur, Feroze had been consumed with taking forward his father's political legacy, and Bina had focused on her studies, earning a scholarship in a medical college in Lahore on minorities' seats. Their communication had dwindled to a great extent. They were not kids anymore who would make stories about passing cars.

Besides, what would father say?

"Feroze, I talked to you yesterday about Sharda as well. It's been a week she's missing. Now they have released some fake statement that she went on her own. Did you talk to uncle about it?"

"How do you know it's fake, Bina?"

His voice had assumed a peremptory tone that Bina wasn't used to.

"Kamla *Bua* says she's not eighteen."

"Bina, I checked the documents. They clearly state her age to be eighteen."

"Feroze, Kamla *Bua* cannot even tell between the scripts of Sindhi and Urdu. And she does not even remember getting Sharda's birth registered. She was born in Kashmir, and they remained in the valley for two months. No one bothered about the documentation then. You know many of the people here still don't."

"So you are taking your illiterate maid's word against mine?"

Bina took a moment to conserve her poise and not dissipate the unbridled anger at Feroze.

"She is not our maid, Feroze, and all I am asking you is to talk to your father. You know he can help."

"I will, Bina."

"Thank you, Feroze. We are very worried here."

"But Bina, it's very convenient that you call me out of the blue after being absent. You don't keep in touch anymore."

The greatest human tragedy.

To cross the lines that have already been drawn.

"I know, Feroze, I have only been busy with my medical studies. I told you the same when we met in Lahore. . ."

Silence.

But then, what was there to conclude about time and actions? What was surmountable and what was not? What was defensible and what was not?

The age of Sharda Peeth: 2000 years.

The age of Pakistan: 75 years.

The age of Sharda: sixteen or eighteen years, depending on who you asked.

* * *

She called the next day again, desperation giving way to furious anxiety.

"Feroze, did you talk to your father? What does he say?"

"Bina, I talked to him. He told me the girl went of her own will."

He had talked to his father; that part was true, but the reply had been different. Hashmatullah's reply was something between, "Is my son now becoming an activist for Hindu girls, ha!" and "You really think I owe you any answers?"

And the Gorgon had smiled right then.

Bina lost it, she snarled at Feroze.

"Feroze, are you out of your senses? One minor Hindu girl has been forcibly converted and married off to an old Muslim man at the behest of a man who's your father's political ally, and you are telling me their fake version of the story?"

The Gorgon woke up, raised her head, thought for a moment, and went back to sleep.

"Bina, you're just overreacting. Two adults got married, did with their religions whatever they wanted to do; what's your problem here?"

"My problem is you're all lying. Sharda was gearing up for her exams. Kamla *Bua* had spent all her life ensuring she gave her a proper education. You know what my equation with Sharda is; she is my sister. You've met her, Feroze; you know her. She wasn't on the lookout for old men of your faith to get married to."

"People do what they do, Bina. And people convert for the people they like."

"She is a kid. For fuck's sake, she is a kid."

"You would have also converted were we to get married."

"What???!"

On a Neem tree beside the Grand Trunk Road that passes through Sukkur and leads to Karachi, a bird got stuck in a wire hanging loose from one of its branches. It tried to break free, but the effort grazed the wire around its neck. It fluttered for a while, and died.

"You're not the person I knew, Feroze. You have turned out to be the problem, not the solution we talked about. Remember when we talked about the diversity of our mother Sindh, and our friendship was a testimony to that? Remember when you used to say you don't aspire to be a typical politician because you will never sell your soul? Remember the stories you used to make about a pluralistic empire you'll be running one day? Today, men of your faith are forcibly converting minor girls of mine, and you are defending them? Can you even imagine the pain their parents must be going through? What happened to you?"

If Shabbaraat were here, he could not have been able to tell where the father ended, and the son began listening to Feroze's reply.

"Come on, Bina. You're an adult; come out of those childhood stories and stop playing the victim card already. You act as if you're in trouble here, but have you seen what your people are doing to Muslims in India? They are killing them daily, lynching and maiming them. Burning their places of worship. It's a genocide happening there. Yesterday, it was Babri. Tomorrow, it will be what, the Taj Mahal? Come off your high horse and open your eyes!"

Bina felt a stinging cold sweeping into her bones. Everything said after "your people" was an inaudible, insulting echo to her.

My people.
Your people.
My country.
Your country.
That side of the line.

Feroze took only half a moment to realise what he had done. He was shocked at where the words came from. They weren't his. They had never been his.

They come from the study downstairs, the Gorgon laughed.
The legacy of the father.
The sins of the father.

Feroze might have apologised the next moment, but Bina's voice came from the other side of the phone, unrecognizable. It was then that the Bina Feroze had always known was gone.

"Oh my God, Feroze, *pahnjo hee pee lago payo aahein*," she said in Sindhi.

"You have become your father, Feroze."

She cut the phone.

All his life, Feroze had longed to hear these words.

But now that they came, they sounded different from how they did in Feroze's mind - like an allegation in place of adulation.

Around them, time continued moving, observing all but waiting for none.

The age of Bina and Feroze's impending disconnect: eleven years.
The age of Sharda: officially eighteen.

* * *

Right then, about a thousand kilometres to the north, some distance off Muzaffarabad, in the village of Sharda in Neelum Valley, a group of schoolboys, after bunking their classes, made their way to the ancient structure that stood there for many, many years. In countries like ours, vandalism is also a past-time. The boys started a competition by hitting the temple with rocks. The one who hit the highest would win, but if the rock flew over the temple, it would lead to disqualification. After twenty minutes, the winner was decided. The boys sat against a wall of the temple to rest. One of them then picked up a stray rock and rubbed it hard against the wall of the roofless temple, etching a deep line on a stone.

Chapter Eleven

"**THERE ARE** some rules of living in this country, Feroze. In fact, living is an overstatement; surviving should be more like it. And rules are rules; if you try revising them, they'll destroy you. You should do well to remember these."

"Yes, baba."

"The four rules of survival in this country are:

1) Might is right.
2) Who knows whom.
3) Give and take.
4) Push and pull."

"Yes, baba." It was as if the secret to eternity had been divulged to Feroze. *Aab-e-Hayat:* the elixir of life; it made Feroze immortal. It was the first time his father was treating him like a man. This was his emancipation. A father sharing factual information with his son was the second most intimate form of welcoming the latter into manhood by the former in this part of the world. The first was sharing the pain, which Feroze would never know as his father steered clear from that sort of confiding. The fourteen-year-old Feroze took all the rules in thoughtfully, remembered them and, in his mind, improved and accentuated them as he was to carry baba's legacy. He should be efficient and always willing to put in the extra effort. Feroze's mindful modification altered the rules only slightly.

1) More might is more right.
2) Who actually knows whom in what capacity.
3) Give a lot and take more than a lot.
4) Push hard, pull harder.

"And Feroze, there's only one law in this country. There's no getting away from it; if you try otherwise, you're fed to the dogs in the dungeons. You ought to remember this."

"What is that, baba?" Feroze's excitement aviated on realising his father had more to give him; clearly, he had roused that confidence in him.

"Either fuck, or get fucked."

***

Hashmatullah Khan's little kingdom impressed all his peers, even if it was more about building on his father's legacy than espousing his own ideals. But what Nasrullah had achieved in his life, Hashmat had augmented that ferociously, functioning largely without any compass of propriety and morality.

But morality is a subjective thing.

"Morality is the howl of the weak, Feroze. It's for the middle classes. Morality is just as good as communism, the old woman's cries of having failed to manoeuvre successfully through the system. A man has to protect his family, which is how he is defined. You've got to do what you've got to do for yourself and your family."

You've got to do what you've got to do.

Feroze now had five rules.

Not that all of Hashmat's you've-got-to-do-what-you've-got-to-do was met with applause. His yarns were often the talk of the town, at least in the English dailies of the province, even when the

Sindhi ones bowed before him in a show of explicit endorsement. Some of these criticisms were safely guarded by Hashmat in his study; Feroze had found some while scampering through the room when his father was absent: to find a piece of his father he had forgotten behind. Feroze would adopt it in a second.

Some newspaper clippings carried images of a younger Hashmat, with headlines that screamed impolite words.

"Sindhi leader joins the military dictator in an impudent show of power hunger."

The news item read, "The renowned Sindhi leader Hashmatullah Khan has decided to support the military dictator in his sabotage of power. This move was seen as controversial by the other parties and some factions of his own party, as it contradicted his stern affirmation of promoting democracy in the country. Hashmat, whose late father Nasrullah also served as a member of the provincial assembly, originally belonged to Punjab…."

Feroze would take this news with a snigger: *the cry of the weak.* Clearly, the newspaper editors were jealous of his father. Feroze could make a mental note of his father's response: "This country is not fit for democracy. How do you give democracy to a horde of sheep? And where are the Pakistan Movement leaders anyway? The Lahore resolution was passed by people belonging to areas that are now in India, and when they couldn't leave their Kanpurs and their Lucknows for their great idea of Pakistan, what are we bleating about? They talk about democracy and equality and give us examples of Land Reforms in India. What is the equality they are talking about? That the failures in life be put on the same pedestal as the winners? This is the second martial law in this country, and its success has already shown all of us what it means to run this country. Democracy is for established countries, not for stinking potholes…."

That is how a son would routinely defend his infallible, towering father; without realising that the father would never have a need to do the same. The newspaper the child read was the original edition his father had procured. Before going into print, the item criticising his father had been duly whitened by the martial law administrator's watchdogs.

But the real problem was there wasn't one narrative to justify. Hashmatullah's posture changed with the hour. While denouncing democracy landed him in the good books of the dictator, Hashmat was also the first to jump ship as the dictatorship's hold thinned out. He would then retreat to canvassing for votes on the lone conviction that democracy was the only thing the country needed, and that it was a shame that some powers always hijacked the process. He would one day be affirming his faith in the secular character of Sindh, while opting to be in bed with the extremist forces on another.

Hashmatullah's ideology could not be neatly put down to a simplistic reason. What fuelled his actions could be a myriad of justifications, but most stemmed from the concept of power, and the fear it comes with. The fear of not *fully* belonging, the fear of being an outcast, the fear of retribution. Whatever he did was rarely out of a malignant volition for others but only to attend to his own dread. And like an afraid power, Hashmatullah had always made wise choices. He had always chosen to fuck.

* * *

After his father's death, the laws and rules had also started relaxing their grip on Feroze's mind - first taking a back seat over the nape of his neck, then flowing through his spine and escaping. Reading his grandfather's diaries enabled Feroze to humanise his family, even if the logs did not have much to offer in terms of content. At most, they were tense, sculling in Feroze a curiosity to know more about the father who cried for his books, and the settlement they had over the land with Bina's ancestors. Feroze had never really known that their family had migrated; for him, they were always here. To know that his lineage carried impressions of a complicated past he could never secure access to wasn't the most gratifying thing to him. He yearned to delve into the details; if only there was a way to talk to dead people.

Feroze sat in his room, wondering if meeting Bina's father would be a good idea. He decided against it instantly, there evidently was bad blood between his father and him, and he never got to know why. It had, anyway, been ages since Feroze had met his uncle Vankwani. Feroze gazed into the distance. Two fruits fell on the ground on a *Jamun* tree in front of his house. One crashed against the tree's root and got stuck; the other bounced off a turn in a twig and landed a little distance away. One did not get light and died; the other made its roots into the soil and would start growing in a couple of weeks.

* * *

Feroze removed the statue of the Gorgon from the lounge some months after his father's death; his mother surprisingly did not make a show of it. He was told by their family doctor that she was suffering from post-traumatic disorder, and her treatment had been started. The crack that emerged in this father's death and mother's illness brought in a ray of light. Feroze seized it and retired the Gorgon to the store. As a kid, he was always scared of it (even if it was from Belgium).

This was one way to do away with the inheritance of silence.

Feroze's mind became a labyrinth: of questions that did not have answers, of feelings that he did not know could be regrets, of repentance at not having bounced off a twig of a tree, but landing in the wretched shadows of another.

He started spending most of his time in his father's library, so much so that many of his meals would also be served there. He dived in books, reports, recordings, recollections, letters, memorandums, anything that could be found inside moth-eaten covers and half-torn pages. It was battering; he did not know what to make of anything. He was stuck deciphering the contrast between his image of his father and who his father had actually been. Feroze did not realise that the undoing he was to do regarding the legacy thrust upon him would also be his own undoing.

It was the fight of one against one's self.

Where does one begin and the other end?

It is a continuum.

Feroze was obsessed; he got sick in the process but did not let this tirade go astray. He spent days ingesting everything he got, not digesting all but striving to.

And instead of the answers he was looking for, he was greeted with more questions. It was like throwing a huge net into the River Indus and only getting a few fish. Every day would come with a new stupor, the crack now opening so much that the light it allowed to enter was now blinding.

Why had Shree uncle and baba stopped talking, given that grandfather had written they were friends?

Why was Bina afraid to be seen with him?

Were all the newspaper reports right?

Were Aariz and Bina right?

Was his father not really the man he thought?

What did he think anyway?

Whose thoughts were they anyway?

The Gorgon smiled from inside the store.

Feroze eventually gave up. If he wanted to ask his father anything, he wouldn't be able to. If he tried to fight his ghost, he would only wound himself.

But on the spectrum of either-fuck-or-get-fucked, Feroze did not know where he had been all his life.

* * *

One a night when fog was rehearsing to take the city over, Feroze called Shabbaraat up to his room. This wasn't frequent, to the point of being rare. The younger *sahab* seldom talked directly to the servants. All the directions concerning him would be communicated to the servants by the lady of the house. The old servant had been sceptical at first; what if the son also does to him what his father had? The limp in his walk that had been recovered by years of unwavering practice again registered itself. His wife cried; she still remembered the force of the potent kick the late master had once offered her. But Shabbaraat went; he did not have any other option anyway. His old body might not be able to take it anymore, but his mind had been conditioned to hostility all these years.

You've got to do what you've got to do.

When Shabbaraat entered the room, knocking carefully, he saw Feroze sitting on the floor, sucking a burning cigar and dropping the ash on the wooden floor. His eyes were swollen, but probably not due to tears as they spoke of a lack of sleep. He motioned him towards himself, telling him to sit on the study table chair. Shabbaraat was hesitant at first. Was it a ruse? But even if it was, there was no escape. He sat slowly, worrying about what was to come next.

Feroze looked at him for a while and, with a trace of a faint smile, said, "Tell me about my father!"

Shabbarrat looked back at him, his mouth quivering in inelegant directions, and he started, "Your father was a great man, *sahabjee*. He..."

"TELL ME ABOUT MY FATHER!" Feroze growled, looking at him as if his sight would sear the skin of the old servant, not blinking; the temperature in the room soared by four degrees.

Shabbaraat knew the time for beating around the bush was over. If truth would cost him his life, so would not telling the truth. There wasn't really a lesser evil for him there.

And he started, right from when Nasrullah had brought over Shabbaraat as a kid, and through all the years hence.

That night, the two men conversed till dawn, most of it being a monologue. And they talked in detail about the man who had died and what he had left behind.

The legacy of the father.

And all that he had done in his life.

The sins of the father.

Chapter Twelve

AARIZ OFTEN sought an opportunity to meet Mehar; now that her phone was in her custody, she would always reply. He always felt a whiff of warmth run through him whenever her name would flash on his phone's screen. Mehar had not confided in him any details about her ended marriage, and this strangely piqued Aariz. She owed that much to him, at least. But Mehar was incorrigible. Their phone communication had been suspended during the initial years of her marriage. Aariz hadn't left for Dubai back then, and he once asked Bina to arrange a meet-up. Bina had ended the topic without using many words.

In the first year of shifting abroad, Aariz was once disrupted from a meeting by the vibration of his phone.

It was Mehar.

He had rushed out of the meeting hall, excusing all the other participants, and found an empty lobby in the hotel to take the call.

"Mehar?" his voice disrupting all the molecules hovering around the air from Dubai to Lahore.

First, there was silence, then the sound of a muffled cry.

It lasted only a minute, and the call went dead.

After that, nothing. Up until the day when a divorced Mehar returned to the Old City.

* * *

"Hello Mehar, is our plan still on?"

"Yes, Aariz. Even though I have told you that Shahdara is not the area included in your consultancy services."

"I know, but I think the old Mughal monuments might give me another angle to the renovation of this area." The lie was unconvincing. He couldn't care less about the Mughal monuments.

Mehar smiled.

She knew.

"I will meet you at two outside the Delhi Gate. Don't come inside. People like you are conspicuous here."

Aariz read the reply and smiled.

And then there is Mehar.

* * *

Mehar had to wait for a while in the shade of the *Khatm-e-Nabuwat* banner that hung loose in front of Delhi Gate, which announced that Ahmadis were apostates and any business activity with them was forbidden. Mehar was covering her face, hoping not to be recognised by any familiar faces that darted across her. Shama had asked her where she was going, and she had used Nashmia, like she had on so many occasions before. She did not even have to inform Nashmia about this. She was sure Nashmia would pull off an incredibly compelling show of pretence would the opportunity arise. Once, when Mehar had gone out with Bina during her medical college days, telling her sister-in-law about Nashmia, Shama had called the latter. Nashmia had no idea about the whereabouts of Mehar, but she told Shama that Mehar was sitting in the lobby of her house. She called Mehar's name, and distancing the phone from her mouth, she mimicked a "jee" in Mehar's voice.

Mehar's brother was not at home, and Shama had not asked any further questions; she had this daily soap to watch, and it would be a shame if she were to redirect her attention from what was happening on the TV to what was happening in her sister in law's life.

And a lot was happening in her sister-in-law's life.

A storm was brewing.

It was the storm that ensues in the wake of enlightenment, testing your capacities before unshackling the throes of existence. Like the storm that tested a Gautama's resolve as he sat beneath a Bodhi tree.

Mehar had wanted to tell Bina that this storm had been brewing for a long time. It started brewing many years ago when Bina introduced her to this male friend of hers. It was there when she was forced out of her house to take in the hostility of a man through her body. It had continued to howl even when she was beaten and abused by her husband. It had kept on roaring even when she catered to her husband's friends every night.

You were really enjoying yourself with Mujtaba tonight, you slut!

Why were you acting like a piece of dead animal with Siraj, manhoos!

She nudged the memories off at once, but they would often come despite all her barricades. They had been engraved so deeply in her mind that they now constituted a monument in her head. And there were enough monuments in the Old City already. And she was to take Aariz to some that day, who still had not appeared.

When Aariz finally came into her view, wearing a white, starched shalwar kameez to go with the character of the place they were to go to, they pretended not to notice each other. One had learned the ways of functioning in the Old City, and the other had been duly taught. They walked towards the north, keeping a safe distance between them, and Mehar hinted towards a rickshaw driver that screeched in front of her. She made a deal with a rickshaw driver and sat in it. Aariz followed.

* * *

Fifteen minutes later, they were crossing the dilapidated bridge across the River Ravi, or Iravati as Bina always called it. Aariz was visibly uncomfortable and sat on the edge of the seat. The rickshaw entered minuscule, tiny spaces to the shock of Aariz, compounded by the army of motorcycles and tongas that closed in from all directions at random. The rickshaw driver would hit his foot on the accelerator with a sense of vindication and took snappy turns that rattled Aariz.

"Does he even have a driver's license?" he asked Mehar.

"What is that?" Mehar smiled.

After a while, when Aariz's vigilance hadn't shown any signs of abatement, Mehar comforted him, "Relax, it's the survival of the fittest on these roads."

"More like the survival of the rashest."

About another fifteen minutes of Aariz's endless concerns later, they ascended the staircase of a minaret of Jahangir's tomb. The bumpy rickshaw ride had even sent those of Aariz's body parts protesting which he didn't know formerly existed, and going atop the staircase was an exercise for him. Mehar was untouched by all of it. She was used to everything. They had gotten off the rickshaw, where Mehar had again taken the lead to buy tickets for both of them. The ticket seller had looked at Aariz.

"Foreigner? Not 20, 200 rupees."

Mehar had said something in indistinct Punjabi, and they entered the complex.

It was a grand complex that fanned out on multiple grounds. They had emerged in the centre of the compound, where rooms surrounded all the sides. Mehar had headed straight, then turned right. As they emerged from the gate in that direction, the tomb of a Mughal Emperor came into their view. Aariz had never been to this place before; Mehar was his only source of reference there.

Aariz and Mehar first went to the grave, took their shoes off, and said Fatiha (only Mehar, not Aariz). Then Mehar had shone the light of her phone on a gemstone engraved on the emperor's tomb, and the stone became a dazzling spectacle. Aariz smiled.

They came out, and Mehar paid something to the security guard on duty. He took it without a word and opened the lock on the gate that opened on the rooftop of the tomb, where four minarets presented their individual set of stairs to be mounted.

When they reached the top of the minaret, Mehar took a deep breath and took in the view that opened to them in all directions. She looked at the city. Aariz looked at her. Mehar sat on the floor, putting her weight on the lattice marble screen surrounding the nifty space. Aariz followed suit.

The wind blew from all directions, ruffling Mehar's hair and Aariz's heart.

"So, what do you want to know?"

"Everything."

* * *

As a child, Mehar often visited the old Mughal buildings in the area. She would sneak out of her house on crazy summer afternoons when everyone was asleep, tag along with her friends from the muhalla (Hadi, Toor, and sometimes Nashmia), and take them to some old place to play. The kids sweated in the heat, lost their colours in the sun, and invited their parents' rage, but were resolute. Mehar would find a sense of solace in these old buildings that she wouldn't in her immediate world. She started gathering details of all these buildings from anyone willing to share them. She lured the guards into telling her stories about the places, which they often did but with extreme misinformation. She would take in the architectural details of a building as if she had a degree in architecture. She would often engender stories about these, knowing the kids she hung out with were easy targets to be fooled.

"This building is built in the Roman style. And as you know, Rome was not built in a day."

"How many days was it built in, Mehru?" Toor would ask.

"Rome or this building?"

"This building."

"In a thousand days."

"And Rome?"

"In two thousand days, as it is a bigger building!"

She would awe at an ancient building, relating herself to it in ways she could only explain to herself.

She would become Noor Jahan, and look at Jahangir's tomb with the precise eye of a builder.

"If only the central building were higher, they would not have called it the second most magnificent Mughal structure, but the first."

She would become Ladli Begum in Noor Jehan's tomb, and inquire her mother about not being buried with her husband.

"It's a shame the whole tomb only has one person buried."

She would become Dilaram in the Fort's Paaen Baagh, and plot against Jahangir's favourite courtesan.

"I will send Nadira to where she came from."

She would become the Mughal princess Jahan Ara and observe the water flushing like pearls down the fountains in Shalimar Bagh.

"There were seven grounds to this gardens, while only three remain. I will remake all of them."

She would become Gulrukh Begum in her father Kamran Mirza's baaradari, and judged the people who announced their love, replete with drawing hearts and their phone numbers by scratching the walls.

"Crush these miscreants under elephants!"

As Mehar grew older, she also learned some real stories, even if the real in them was still marred in places by fantasy. And those are the stories she told Aariz that day, without an interlude and keen consideration of his interest.

She told him that you could only see three minarets of the Badshahi Mosque from any of the minarets of Jahangir's tomb, and vice versa. One minaret of either structure always fell in one line if sighted from the other. She told him that no one knew what was buried inside the tomb, as Jahangir and his wife were at odds with where the emperor would want to be buried. One wanted to be buried in Kashmir, and the other decided Lahore for him. The body of the dead emperor was then opened up and divided: flesh in Kashmir and bones in Lahore. She told him that Noor Jahan was afraid of the dark, and she willed to be hanged in her tomb instead of being buried. She also designed her tomb so that windows at the ground level bring light to her underground grave at sunrise and sunset each day. But then the Sikhs came, opened the hanging coffins, looted all the jewels, and buried the remains inside the soil. She also told him stories about long-disappeared tunnels that once connected Lahore to Delhi, and ran between here and there.

Aariz was amused at this downpour of information.

"You really know a lot about these places."

"I have lived with them."

I am them.

She continued, "I visited these often when I was little. Then I grew up, and they started haunting me. And all I wanted to do was to leave."

"And which monument haunts you the most?"

"My own."

Mehar got up, and assumed the position where the city stretched across her in a panorama. She saw that one of the gates of the mausoleum was in physical contact with the houses of the people who had hence made Shahdara their home; it was a question of only one jump for them to change their location from the present into the past. When they were all children, Mehar, Hadi and Toor had once entered the upper room of this gate, escaping the prying eye of the guard on duty. There, they had found strange stuff: discarded items of clothes that are worn under the clothes, household garbage and plastic waste, and transparent rubber thrown in the corners. Mehar had never seen such a balloon before, but Hadi and Toor had started laughing on seeing it, infuriating

Mehar. In her mind, the monuments were hers, and it was a shame the boys around her understood something about what lay in them that she didn't. Presently, Mehar smiled and faced the other angle of the view: a thin trickle of water stuffed with industrial effluents remained the sole fragment of the river that had dried up. It provided a preamble to a city that had kept on increasing in size and population since it was born - like a malignant tumour. She could spot a never-ending array of squat houses, doors, buildings, and people. "How many doors and windows are there in the city of Lahore?" Someone had asked Bulleh Shah four centuries ago. "And how many bricks in the city are firm, and how many are broken? And how many wells have fresh water, and how many have salty? And how many women in Lahore are married, and how many are single?" Baba Bulleh Shah had waited for a while before answering, pondering, and then he said, "I will tell you what lies in the city of Lahore. There are millions of windows, as are millions of doors. The bricks that carry the memories of lovers' footprints are broken, and the rest are firm. The wells that have quenched a lover's thirst have fresh water, while all the others have turned salty. And only the women who sit with their lovers are married, and all the rest are single."

Mehar turned towards Aariz. And then, she also told him "everything" as he had asked.

Chapter Thirteen

THE MALL road in Lahore snakes through the colonial underpinnings of the city, marked on both sides by several buildings that speak of geometrical precision and an invader's print. Many of the buildings have since been demolished; they had refused to carry the burden of the legacy anymore. Many have given in themselves; they couldn't bear the sins of others. But many still stand: some as museums, some as government offices, others as housing emblems of consumerism. Interestingly, some buildings and some people seem to be in a sort of naked competition with each other when it comes to resilience. They burn at both ends - cracked, broken, rotten - but do all there could be done to evade death. The fear of the great unknown is still a more significant deterrent for them than the fear of being undone.

Nothing kills them. Nothing makes them stronger.

It's the dance of survival.

Gasping, out-of-synch, but right on the beats.

Tick. Tick. Tick.

There's a separate Lahore for each of its historical periods. The ancient Lahore. The Mughal Lahore. The Sikh Lahore. The Colonial Lahore. The Modern Lahore. It clearly wasn't invaded only once during its history.

La-whore.

It had opened up to everyone.

Lahore's history is a string of endless invasions; it's difficult to tell where one ends, and the other begins.

***

At three in the morning, the demons wake up in a sleeping city.

The statue of Queen Victoria in the Museum starts crying, slowly pacing up. "Help me out! I don't belong here. I lived on the road there; who caged me inside?"

The red bricks of the General Post Office start chuckling, "She does not see what we see. She does not belong anywhere anymore. And there's nothing to see anyway."

Azadi, Azadi, the chants grow stronger from Charing Cross; they rumble throughout the area.

"Fire," General Dwyer orders from across some miles. Gunshots go up in the air. Body parts jump into the skies.

Bhagat Singh laughs, *"Mera Rang De Basanti Chola."* Colour my cloak saffron. *"They cannot break me. But whose hero am I?"*

Qutb Ud Din Aibak comes out of his grave, "Where is my Minar? What has happened here? How long have I been sleeping for?"

Azadi, Azadi, some people have joined in from Qissa Khawani in Peshawar, their fresh blood dripping.

May our tribe grow; a bearded old man looks at them and laughs. They embrace.

"Dogs," Edwina says, "It was never a good idea to come here. Oh, how I miss London."

Some dead people open their eyes in the corridors of King Edward University and go dead again.

A well, off Montogemery road, swells up and spits; breast-slashed bodies of thirteen women come out. "They couldn't dishonour us."

Anarkali wakes up in her chamber in the Secretariat. "Was I ever alive? Was I a conspiracy? What was I? What are these documents piled over me?"

The building of the Tollinton Market shakes a little, and two pictures hanging in its hall fall to the ground. "Good riddance."

Azadi, azadi.

"Can you send my daughter's dead body to Mr. Radcliffe, please? He'll enjoy it." A man wearing a turban asks the headless guard at the gate of the National College of Arts.

Simmons, Crisps, and Minto shake hands before the Masonic Temple, "When did this place become a dry country? Where do we get brandy now?"

A train to Pakistan unloads inside Wagah. Several formless creatures come out and lay in a line on the Thandi Sarak, arranging their hanging parts covered in blood in a fine line. "Finally, we are home!"

Azadi, azadi.

All hail our liberator; four Bengali men carry a coffin of Winston Churchill.

"But where is our Koh-i-Noor?" someone in a Muslim League gown asks.

Victoria cries louder; she has heard the name of Koh-i-Noor. It's suffocating inside.

Jehangir kicks his tomb, "I wanted to be buried in Kashmir. Why have I ended up here?"

Noor Jehan tearfully looks at her husband from a distance. It has been 400 years since they haven't talked.

Azadi, azadi.

Nehru and Mountbatten look at the enlarging crowds from a distance, each trying to evade the other's glance.

"Your brain goes above your intestine, stupid!" two kids have started fighting about their body parts.

Ghalib drifts across the clouds above, looking at the commotion beneath, "I always liked Delhi anyway."

"Fire," Dwyre shouts again. The men laugh; "we are already dead."

"Indians are not allowed," one Sikh puts a sign on Gymkhana Club. Two other Sikhs rip him up.

Azadi, azadi.

A dead princess wakes up; she tells everyone she is Bamba Sunderland, the last heir of the Sikh Empire. No one listens to her.

A popular musician in a rebellious black saari joins the protestors: *"Kya taaj uchaalay gaye? Kya takht giraaye gaye?"* Have the crowns been tossed? Have the thrones been brought down?

Fakir Azizudin wades past the rioters and goes to the Samadhi of Ranjit Singh: "Good that your left eye is still bad. You are lucky you can see only half of this spectacle."

Azadi, azadi.

A sloganeer asks Faiz to write something; he opens his diary and writes, *"Dard ki anjuman, jo mera des hai."* Congregation of pain, my country.

Dai Anga exits the Gulabi Bagh, weighted down by regret, "I sacrificed my son for Dara Shikoh, but he still didn't become the Emperor."

The queen of melody encourages the mob and puts on a gramophone record, "All of madam jee's songs are for you, *mere naghmay tumharay liye hain.*"

Azadi, azadi.

The bells of the Sacred Heart Cathedral start ringing violently, they shake the ground, but no one goes for prayers.

Professor Woolner sees that his is the only statue still on the Mall Road, and finds company in the *Gora* Qabristan.

The Mughal building of the Punjab Public Library collapses a little into the ground, "No one reads books anymore."

Azadi, azadi.

Chandra Shekar Azad roams around the area, agitated, "Where did I shoot Saunders?"

The slogans get louder. The cries grow shriller. *"Britishers, go back!"*

The gun is still there; Kipling looks at it and chortles.

Gangaram shouts, "Don't destroy my city; it's taken me a lifetime to build it."

"But what is there to save?" Buddha calls from the Museum.

GulabDeviholdsGangaram'shandandtakeshimtoGangaram Hospital, "Your portrait has been removed."

Azadi, azadi.

Iqbal, the poet, stays silent, holding his head in his hands.

A group of men, fire in place of eyes, starts fighting. "But we celebrated Lohri together only yesterday!"

I knew all this; Manto sniggers and sleeps on the other side. "Humans, filth!"

A dead radio inside a warehouse off Davis Road turns on itself and announces, "The date is 14th August 1947; this is Radio Pakistan."

"*Pakistan Zindabad!*" a few people shout before they are hounded up by others.

Azadi, azadi, they have started blaring out.

Azadi, azadi, now it's drumming.

Azadi.

Freedom.

But from whom?

But from what?

* * *

Aariz woke up at seven in the morning, soaked in a dense layer of sweat. It was the first day of his new school. The night was edgy for him; he had had a nightmare again, even though he could not recall much except for blood and shouting. He was used to these; it had been long since the nightmares became routine associates of his nights. He, at times, considered that it was only after the passing of Old Papa that they had started tempering with his sleep, but that wasn't right. They might have increased in intensity, and to some extent, in frequency since then, but they pre-dated

Old Papa's death. Lately, many of the characters that marred his nightmares would come from Old Papa's books that Aariz was so fond of reading and the stories he had told him. Old Papa used to say that even as a baby, Aariz would wake up frightened. The practice became so common that Old Papa worried his son might be suffering from seizures.

He thought it could be epilepsy.

But it wasn't.

The EEG came alright; there was no problem. The poor baby was just having bad dreams.

Some babies do.

It was never mentioned that it was probably concerning, and no one was sure what it meant.

When Aariz started talking, he would share all his dreams with Old Papa, or at least all he could recollect, which wasn't much. But Old Papa always managed to convert all the gory details into humorous elements. So Aariz learned to detach the emotion of fear from something that was supposedly fearful. Blood became another colour for him. Scary faces only some creatures from another planet that looked different. He had been sleeping alone for years, and the nightmares never made him skittish. They just disturbed him, as anyone would be by lights and sounds during sleep. He developed a restful equation with things boys his age would not be snug with.

Water and Oil.

Aariz dressed into his new uniform that Mama had hung in his room - all neatly ironed and starched - and went downstairs where Mama was waiting for him. New Papa had already gone to work. Mama kissed Aariz on the cheek and waved at the driver to ready the car, "First day of your new school. You know what papa had to do to get you an admission here! Only a few lucky ones get this opportunity. Be good!"

Aariz sheepishly smiled at her. He felt that Mama had changed after her marriage to New Papa.

Previously, she was always there for Aariz, to the extent of dictating Old Papa on the right kind of parenting. He had seen his parents fight over him, Mama telling Old Papa that his discourse with Aariz was unsuitable for a child. But she had been growing distant ever since Old Papa had gone. Aariz did not like it. Mama was the only physical hook he held on to Old Papa with, and he tried to not let the grip go. At least four times, he had also tried to share with her a troubling thing that he thought might have been important, but she had interrupted him mid-way, shrugged her shoulders, and told him she was busy.

Did she know?

Half an hour later, they turned left on the Mall Road and neared the school.

* * *

The school that sat a little off Lahore's Mall Road was a daunting colonial structure. It was built in the nineteenth century by the British to produce a class of gentrified individuals from the backwaters of India, the "princely elites," as they called them. It had magnanimous grounds, multiple buildings, sports complexes, and uncountable trees that had stood through the times. After the creation of Pakistan, the school had served as the production house of many of its leaders, bureaucrats, and politicians. Getting in the school was exclusive, and the school kept creating further batches of people who were separate from the rest.

Their masters.

Only that they weren't white this time.

Does history repeat itself?

Two boys were dropped off inside the school campus at precisely the same time that day. They got out of their cars and walked inside towards the main hall, where the reception proceedings were to begin. They walked through the gallery, side by side, looking at their side of the wall. It had pictures of numerous important people that had run their country - or destroyed it, depending on who you asked. One boy took it all in without being affected in any way, like a layer of oil sliding past a pool of water. The other boy was mute but visibly impressed, his father had also studied here, and this was his becoming.

These boys would grow into friends in the coming weeks; it would be a friendship that many would awe at. Brothers from different mothers, as other classmates would say, sometimes humorously.

It was the design of the cosmos.

And then, one day, they would stop talking to each other.

The cosmos works in peculiar ways.

* * *

In their school in Lahore, Aariz and Feroze grew to become each other's best friends. Not that there was much in common between them, they were rather different as people; but commonality has never been a beacon of friendships. Feroze was ambitious; he seized every opportunity he could that he supposed would make his father proud. He would always put in extra effort in everything, go the extra mile, and was quick to learn the proper ways of the elites. Aariz was laid back; he was good at everything but did not care much, doing the bare minimum and letting everything else pass. He remained pretty untouched and uninfluenced by the conventions of the world here.

They shared some things in common as well. Both were kind, even if one's idea of kindness was rooted in unkindness not making any reason to him, while the other's came from a place of stature; both were inquisitive about the world around them, even if one's interest was lined by his wonder at the idiocy of it while the other's was driven by a will to conquer; and both shared a quirky reticence that they understood, one bred in himself the anxiety of never making others understand how he felt while the other nurtured a scar for not being able to swing a bat and hit the balls into the pavilion.

One evening, the two boys had an encounter beside a cricket ground in their school. They both stopped to look at its freshly cut grass, sharp enough to give them a little laceration. One boy grieved about how his dead father wasn't with him anymore to chase him around, while the other ruefully recollected how his living father wouldn't like him imitating Saeed Anwar. They looked at each other and pretended there was neither a cricket ground nor memories of their fathers with them. But the curse of destiny was that there were nine cricket grounds in the school.

The boys did not have other options except to learn habitual denial together.

They crossed the fine line from waning childhood to imminent adulthood together, and their friendship only strengthened. Each became a part of the other's extended world as well. On some summer holidays, Aariz would go with Feroze to Sukkur, where he met his friend Bina, whom he talked about a lot and became friends with; on others, they would go abroad on vacation: they went together to Dubai and Nepal. In Lahore, they also shared notes on what was happening in the other's life and assumed they were already a part of it. They spent some years of their lives together, being each other's confidants in the experiences - some of them embarrassing - most people indulge in when the hormones hit them.

They once went on spotting prostitutes in urban Lahore at night. Feroze had heard that some girls acted innocent at the corners of the bustling markets but only revealed themselves when a guy would show interest in them. It was to blow their cover, Feroze convinced Aariz. Aariz termed it "Operation Blow Job" later, and the two boys would cackle about it.

When they tried psychedelics together, they made up stories about who acted weirder under the influence of the drug. Feroze swore Aariz had asserted he was an astronaut and was observing the world only to decide when should be the right time to destroy it. Aariz claimed Feroze had been silent, and then he started crying while singing and dancing to Sindhi songs.

They were there for each other through the stages a boy passes through while becoming a man: anxiety, disturbance, heartbreak, aggression, acceptance.

And habitual denial.

But what distinguished their friendship depended not on being there for each other as much as the absence of expectation from the other to be there in certain circumstances. Only they comprehended the restrictions the other had. And they did not have to justify to each other how one's body and the other's mind worked differently from most.

Their mutual friends often joked that it was difficult for them to spend their lives without each other. They did not know it was untrue; more untrue for one than for the other.

Bina once came to Lahore, before she joined medical college, before she and Feroze had adopted his inheritance of silence, and they all wandered in the city. Later, they met again when Bina joined medical college and brought Mehar along while coming to meet them. It was the only time the four of them had been together in one place; it was probably also the time when Aariz had told them a fascinating story about Lal Shahbaz Qalandar and hell; even if everyone in the group engendered individual equations with everyone else and kept on talking to each other; some more than others.

And then, one by one, cracks started appearing in these bonds.

The cosmos works in peculiar ways.

Chapter Fourteen

AS BINA and Aariz's friendship with Feroze floundered, their friendship with each other fortified. They did keep their tabs on Feroze, though, and gabbed about him often, but decided against any active involvement in his life, ultimately leading to an absolute disconnect. The fact that Feroze also kept tabs on Bina was something that he never got a chance to reveal to her. Bina and Aariz met often; sometimes, Bina would tag along Mehar until the circumstances allowed. Whenever Mehar came, the meeting place would either be their medical college or someplace near Old Lahore; whenever it was just Aariz and Bina, they would discover different eateries in the city, arguably contributing a lot to the local food economy. Bina would often come up with a new quandary, followed by the solution she had envisioned, and stopped only for Aariz to give his tacit agreement to what she was saying. Aariz enjoyed listening to Bina's latest stories of activism, even if he thought her efforts pointless. He knew they wouldn't bear any fruit, much like the efforts of so many others before.

Time is a continuum.

But Aariz rarely said this in front of Bina; he just teased her by saying that she was all sound and fury, signifying nothing. And Bina wasn't the one to be deterred; she was always up to something, and the list of contacts on her phone probably surpassed the cumulative sum of twenty persons'. One day, she'd be gearing up to go to a protest for the restoration of rightful judiciary in the country; on another, she'd be teaming up with a group of documentary filmmakers all set to record the sounds of the Indus. She could often be seen on television, on some local channel talking about the wave of extremism in her province, and would form awareness groups about the nutrition and disease in rural Punjab. Not to mention that her own podcast was one of the most sensible - even if not the most popular - in the country. Despite his reservations about the exercise's effectiveness, Aariz enjoyed Bina going through all this. Her ambition was infectious, it was as if she was out there to change the world. Once, he asked her, "Why do you need to make everything so complicated, Bina? What is the need to contextualise everything?"

"Because there's no solution without addressing the root of the problem."

"No, the solution might be to address the issue you face instead of going deep into the details and taking the debate to a metaphysical level."

"What is this about, Aariz?" Bina was interested.

"I saw your debate on Youtube, in which you were asking about the foundational principle of Pakistan while talking about the issue of feudalism in Sindh."

"So what else would I have done? The thing is, we are looking for answers in black and white. We let go of the nuances, so the point is lost on us. When we aren't settled on whether Muhammad Bin Qasim is our hero or Raja Dahir, failing to reconcile our national and provincial histories, how do you reckon we devise a way forward?"

"Your strategy may lead to more detractors than supporters. If you aim to get things done, you may need to re-think it."

"I don't think trying to clear the confusion is unwise. To titillate debate on something is the first step to understanding a thing. A lot is lost in simplifying and stereotyping. When I talk about forced conversions, do I mean that all minorities in this country are unsafe? No, we live in Sindh normally otherwise, but the popular narrative only focuses on one part. The media picks me up as the Hindu girl inciting war against Pakistan, because that is what we have been fed. I criticise this country because it's mine, and for the potential I see in it. We talk about the provinces as if one lens can give us the full picture. Punjab is way richer than Balochistan. But is a Punjabi peasant more well-off than a Baloch Sardar? If I don't believe that all Sindhi tenants will be out dancing merrily if we get rid of feudalism, does that mean I support the feudal? Things cannot be understood without taking into account the nuances, Aariz. Is class the only real factor underscoring the divide and the oppression here, and do all other factors only act as compounding ones? In the bigger picture, is the two-nation theory all there was to create this country? By that definition, I'm a misfit here and will always be. But you cannot be telling me I don't belong here because this is the land of my forefathers, and where I live like anyone does. Shouldn't we be looking for other explanations as well? For example, the proposition that this creation may also borrow from the fact that the Indus and Ganges civilisation were always distinct? I know that is also contentious, but we need to widen our horizons, and shouldn't someone be asking the real questions?"

"And must that someone be my friend?" Aariz smiled.

"Unfortunately, yes." Bina smiled.

Aariz always supported her, and his encouragement was something Bina relied on. This was constant, except for certain times when Aariz thought Bina was treading upon dangerous territory. Bina would always be tenacious at first, but Aariz succeeded in infusing sense into her. After their daggers drawn at each other for some time, Bina would acquiesce.

"Bina," Aariz would always say when nothing else would work on her. "Let it go. Sometimes, it's folly to be wise."

For her part, Bina loved to hear Aariz's travel stories. He used to travel extensively and would always bring back scintillating stories from places Bina had never been to. When Mehar left medical college, Aariz became the only accessible friend Bina had in the city. Even though Aariz's social circle kept on growing, Bina was irreplaceable. The two friends had stayed in consistent contact even after both left Lahore; Aariz went to Dubai and Bina to Islamabad.

***

While in his college, Aariz took on a part-time job as a feature writer for an English magazine. Much like everything else he did, he turned out to be adequate in it, so much so that his article was turned into a fortnightly segment by the magazine. But Aariz's interest in either writing or travelling did not stem from an actual interest in these activities but from what these activities carried as baggage.

Travelling was his way of connecting to things he could not otherwise connect to; writing was his way of relating to things he found no relevance towards. Through this practice, he started experiencing life through others' lived experiences.

Vicarious living.

He carried the burden of secrets of families that weren't his, being nostalgic about memories he had no right to. It was an escape he treasured.

The secret is to become everything.

***

The more Aariz travelled through the length of his country, the harder it got for him. Because after a certain while, he realised that most places, like most people, are just the same. It's an eternal camouflage everything has shrouded itself in.

You know one, you know them all.

You see one, you see them all.

But Aariz still found himself being sucked in by this exercise.

He also got to shun many misconceptions that people routinely stoked to paint one thing as a monolith and fan the fear of the other. Everything was complicated, even his country. Not that he was ever eager to pass judgements anyway, but travelling in his country made him realise how it was a boiling cauldron of so many ideas and ideals - all finding an oasis of their own to exist in shadows. During his travels through his country, he met all the people a textbook reading of the country told everyone wouldn't exist here. He met atheists and homosexuals, agnostics and apostates, blasphemers and pagans; all found a space in his country that was only theirs, unadulterated. He also made various friends during this time, and some of them maintained consistent contact with him. Saboor, the butcher, who fed the crocodiles in the shrine of Mangho Pir in Karachi every Thursday, and repeated to him the story of how lice had become crocodiles when the Baba had shrugged them off his hair. Qasir Kailasha, the manager of the only four-star hotel in Chitral, who would take Aariz to his house in the Bamburet valley and acquaint him with all the ancient customs his community otherwise protected. Miss Raniya, who had emerged as the first drag queen of Pakistan and was now in a public process of undergoing transition. He could not empathise with others' realities but could understand them. He also understood the massive joke the cosmos had been playing on all of us from infinity. And the play was addictive; generations upon generations of humans had fallen prey to it and had adopted the rules of this game.

Tick, tick, tick.

"The story of the first and the last man on earth will be the same."

Aariz pondered the title for his latest feature article, which had been born from the supplementary observations and stories that made their way to him while he travelled for more practical purposes. Was it too controversial? Will someone point out a tinge of being disrespectful towards organised religion in it? But then again, he was writing for an international magazine in English, and trouble usually brewed only with Urdu. In all of his travels, local and international, there came the point when everything would return to the same point, as if things were on a repeat telecast. People worldwide were laughably similar; it was only by the camouflage of redundant eccentricities that they called themselves different and demanded to be distinct. Indeed, there were differences in how they led their lives. Some washed after catering to the call of nature, and some only used paper and perfume. Some were strict on what to eat and drink, and some downed everything that could be swallowed. Some indulged in pre-marital sex as a routine, while some brayed for blood over it. Some caricatured their holy writings and spun around them comically, while some were eager to kill others for any such misadventure. Some traced their lineage to the female form, while some mutilated the same form in infancy. Some measured the length of what covered their bodies, while some decided to do without any covering. Indeed, there were differences. But even these differences came from the same ideas, the footing remaining one for all. Only the details were different; and that is where God lay, as Old Papa would say.

All the people he met all over the world housed the same notions of birth, love, protection, security, procreation, commitment, vice, virtue, and escape. All would be birthing insecurities and embarrassments, covering it all with a sense of humour and strength, and trying to make sense of everything. And this drudgery of going back to square one led the people in different directions. Due to the frustration of not getting back to the basics, people devised their separate ways. The path was different, but the aim was the same. They were all trying to unveil the magnanimous secret in their own ways.

But what was the secret?

Even the places were the same. After travelling for a while in the world, it wasn't long before Aariz started losing the sense of location. From one angle, he could mistake Scottish farmlands for a Nigerian county. The Himalayas could have been the Alps. Bosphorus would become the South China sea. The Soon Valley would start serving as the preamble of the Grand Canyons. The Sunderbans were the *Amazon*. The palms of Sri Lanka were also in Hawaii.

He knew the cosmos had designed it.

But the cosmos works in peculiar ways, Old Papa had told him.

And it was as if the cosmos had also retired itself from creating content after a while, losing interest in the process. It had started re-using the same people with the same ideas and locations and let them all free to take center stage and carry on with their play.

Even the background music remained the same.

Tick, tick, tick.

* * *

"He carried a thunderbolt in his bludgeoning muscles; he was mighty but also prone to give in to jealousy, love and anger. He impersonated the husband of a woman only to seduce her. He slayed a sea monster. He caused destruction and also brought down thunder and rain. He is Zeus, as the Greeks call him. But he could also be Indra, as per Hindus. It's all a continuum of ideas and stories, and humans have been too hard at getting it. Sitting with any person from any corner of the world and indulging in half a deep discussion with them lays bare the proposition that everything is connected. In pre-historic India, a woman was tricked and abducted by the demon Raavana. He took her to Lanka, and her husband Ram came over to get his wife back - aided by Lakshman. But it wasn't just here that these happenings were unrolled. Helen was abducted by Paris the same way and taken to Troy. Two husbands fought to get their wives back in geographically and chronologically in-contiguous episodes but in eerily similar circumstances. Even the results were similar: the Earth opened and took Sita in. Persephone also disappeared into the Earth.

Adam cried after being sent to the Earth, eager to reunite with Eve. Shiva's tears on the death of Parvati created ponds on Earth. A baby boy is put in a basket and left to float on the river as that is the only way to save him. The boy is given to the layers of the Nile and grows up in Egypt to become Moses. Another river saves another boy who is to be killed. Over the Yamuna, Krishna is sent off to Vrindavan to be adopted by Yashoda. Krishna could only be killed at his ankle; the rest of him was protected. After Gandhari cursed him to die and prayed for the vanquishment of his lineage, a hunter mistook his ankle to be a deer, and hit it with an arrow. Krishna died, but so did Achilles - hit with an arrow on the ankle, which was the only non-immune part of his body. When the Pandavas invited Kauravs to their palace in Hastinapur, the latter couldn't tell whether it was floor or water. And neither could the visitors to Queen Saba's palace, some thousands of kilometres and years away from this place. When the husbands of Draupadi bet her in a game of dice and lost her, the question arose of whether they could have done that, given they had lost themselves already. Shah Mureed also lost Hani to Chakar in the same way, the same cycle of deciding on behalf of a woman, discounting her own standing and will. Humans have always struggled to uphold the truth, whatever their idea of it has been, notwithstanding the price that must be paid. The battleground for truth sometimes becomes Kurushetra, where brothers fight each other for the ideals of rectitude and truth; it sometimes becomes Trojan, where the fight for justice is fought, and culminates in Karbala, where the Imam sacrifices himself in a war against evil. A Mansoor Hallaj is executed in Iraq because he claims he is the truth, and a Heer in Punjab is poisoned on her journey to the truth. And the arrows keep on flowing, sometimes to hurt the lovers, at others to protect them: the arrows of Heracles, Arjuna, Feng Men, Cupid, and Sahibaan. And the winds of time keep blowing over the holy miraculous mountains - Olympus, Kailasha, Wutai, Safa, Marwa - watching them over, only stopping to let the floods of destruction undo all that man has done: sometimes it's the flood of Noah, or that of Manu, or that of the GunYu. As the cycle of destruction and retention continues, we preserve certain emblems to remember things by, even if they are to come again. Devotees go to touch the hand of Guru Nanak carved in stone in Hassanabdaal, processions are held to carry around the tooth of Buddha in Kandy, and people flock every day to see the imprint of the foot on a holy mountain in Sri Lanka. It could be Adam's, or Ram's, or Buddha's, or St. Thomas'…."

Aariz took a break and looked over cursorily at what he had written.

Clearly, it needed to be redone, and he would edit it later. He felt a bit overwhelmed by bringing forth this much; he wasn't sure if he could make any pattern. It was too much of an abstract idea to write about: the human existence as a continuum trying to unravel the mysteries of its being by drawing historical and mythological comparisons. He had succeeded to some extent, he thought.

He scribbled another line that would serve as the article's conclusion after adding more to it: "So the life of the first and the last man on Earth will essentially be underscored by the same effort: a pilgrimage. Everyone ought to take a pilgrimage through time, through people, through ideas, through space, and through self. We are all pilgrims, all bound to the sacred journey of finding the secret of our existence, of our purpose. So what is the secret, then? Could it be to become everything?"

* * *

Aariz often jogged in Lawrence Gardens whenever he was in Lahore. It was something he took after Old Papa. Even with many other parks in Lahore, Lawrence was the duo's favourite. Now rechristened Bagh-e-Jinnah, it reminded Aariz of London. And this connection wasn't a faux pas: the garden had been designed by the British in Lahore because they missed London's Kew Gardens. In Lawrence, Aariz felt influenced by the strings the place carried, an experience he enjoyed. It led him to connect with all the affairs of the places he had seen in the world: not immersing him but only running through him.

Water and oil.

He started jogging.

Beads of sweat appeared on his forehead, spanning in rivulets across his brow – these lanes and alleys of a Brazilian favela – and dripped off the contours of his chin; the cracking of a Colonial building on the Mall road. He ran beside the Weeping Willows, their branches stooping with the load of history's immense legacy, and the veins in his forearms protruded – London tube running smoothly across these sleek tracks. He continued jogging, and the Quaid-e-Azam library, his sole sense of direction in this park of various gates and winding lanes, greeted him past. He gulped some water down his throat, or has the troubled city of Jaffna braced another unwonted monsoon spell? Squirrels darted playfully across the Jamun trees, his gaze following them in the advancing facade of the world through the centuries. He passed the shrine of Baba Turat Murad Shah, eagerly frequented by those hoping to get married, and stopped just there to catch his breath. He inhaled, just as he did when he saw the Northern lights in Lapland. He exhaled, visibly exasperated at Thai spas offering him girls for the night. The sun was about to set, and the hills of the garden erupted in a fiery hue of orange; the same rays silhouetting these palms would soar behind the Eiffel tower on another day. Following the activity, his heart beat fast, like that of a gazelle being chased by a lion in Masai Mara.

And then he felt he missed a beat.

What is the secret?

To become everything?

Or nothing?

Chapter Fifteen

2:00 pm: Hi Aariz. How're you doing? Feroze wanted to meet. I'll be in Lahore next week, planning the meet-up then. I don't know if I want to meet him alone. Will it be possible for you to come as well? I'll ask Mehar to join us as well.

2:30 pm: Hey, doc! I don't have an issue. It's been ages I haven't seen him, so it sounds good.

2:35 pm: Great, Aariz, thank you! And if I may ask, have you forgiven him?

2:37 pm: Who are we to forgive anyone, B?

* * *

2:01 pm: How's my Mehru?

2:04 pm: All good, Bina. You tell? Cannot wait to see you in Lahore.

2:05 pm: Same. I will be there next week. Also, Mehar, can you join us for a meet-up we're planning?

2:07 pm: Who's going to be there?

2:08 pm: Me, you, and Feroze. Have also texted Aariz, he hasn't replied yet, but I'm sure he'll also come.

2:11 pm: Okay, Bina.

* * *

5:00 pm: Hello Feroze. We are meeting next week at Cafe Utopia in Lahore. I'll text you the exact time, but it will be evening. Mehar and Aariz will be there as well.

5:06 pm: GREAT!

Chapter Sixteen

WHILE AGE had failed to meddle with Aariz's appearance, for the most part, it had settled to mate with dissonance and wreak havoc on his mind. For this reason, it was now difficult for him to recall how exactly Feroze looked. He could place the basics, of course, but he would fail to draw from his memory the details of the formation (and that is where God lay). The power to see between the lines and pleats of a face was a prerogative only intimacy afforded to some people, which was long gone between the friends. It had been so many years, almost centuries.

After studying together in the school for four years, Aariz chose to live a different life, replete with a new college - and house. But the friends stayed in contact, at least for the initial years. The city of Lahore remained the common string connecting them, and it was there both had their higher education as well, even if it was in front of a computer for Aariz. Then, largely due to what life entails - the friends started growing apart, their lives leading them to diverging paths.

One's pilgrimage became internal, the other's, external.

For the roughly eight years that followed their school, Aariz and Feroze continued to meet or at least kept in consistent contact. And one day, it changed.

The last time they met was in Lahore; it was three days before Aariz was going to Dubai.

Feroze had come with his father to Lahore at that time for some official business, and he came to meet Aariz after dropping the man to a house in Government Officers Colony.

"Check out my new SUV," Feroze couldn't arrest his excitement.

Aariz patted his back and smiled at the sleek back vehicle that reflected the day's sheen.

Feroze continued, uninterrupted, "I might get a ticket in the next elections. Father says it is my time to take over for him. I might as well be one of the youngest MPAs in the history of Sindh." The recent election was held in the country just a little more than a year ago, and Hashmatullah had again been elected as a member of the provincial assembly of Sindh.

Aariz listened silently. He wanted to say, "then what, how does it matter?" but only smiled.

Everything is a performance.

He felt enraged at Feroze for decimating himself. He also felt sorry for his pitiful state; clearly, Feroze couldn't see it through.

Hashmatullah had recently been involved in a scandal of trafficking Nepali girls to Karachi. It had made the news all around, talk shows saw emotionally charged anchors fuming through their noses, and the country's social media almost succeeded in the virtual revolution it started, but much like everything else in the country, it had died down in a matter of weeks. The inside scoop was that Feroze was a major party to that process. He had worked out all the logistics while feigning ignorance and chose to look the other way since he had become accustomed to accommodating his father's view of the world benevolently.

If survival is an instinct, denial is its greatest aid.

But no one brought it up in the conversation.

They knew.

Feroze asked Aariz about his plans, to which he replied. Uncle Hashim - another friend of Old Papa - was helping Aariz to get the hang of Dubai, and Aariz had already scored a deal with a firm there. Feroze tried to listen intently but couldn't keep the act up in the face of his restlessness. He also brushed over the fact that Aariz was leaving the country indefinitely.

He was getting a ticket, after all.

He never stopped to ask himself if it felt better than playing cricket. Feroze did not ask Aariz about his step-parents; knowing Aariz wouldn't like it, he knew he hadn't seen them since entering college.

They chatted for a long time and talked about the days that only existed in their memories, of long summer days in their school, of coming of age, of life and its incessant surprises that often floor you.

"Remember when we bunked school for the first time, Aariz?"

"You were so scared, Feroze, you peed in your pants." Both laughed.

"If you can come, I'll invite you to Sukkur when the election campaign gears up."

"I always loved being with you in Sukkur, a welcome distraction from the noise of Lahore."

No one can be sure who brought Bina into the conversation first.

"She was telling me about the daughter of her *Bua;* what was her name?"

"Stop it, Aariz! It has been years to that." Feroze's reply was a reflex.

Between being the progeny of his father's ideals and becoming the saviour of a girl, it was anyone's guess what he would choose.

What is defensible and what is not?

"It's just that the court ruled that -"

"You guys are obsessed. Why do you people have to make an issue out of nothing?"

"Relax, brother. I was only saying…"

And then it got personal, "And since when have you started caring about others, Aariz? Is this a way to shame me? I am telling you about what I am going to achieve, and you're bringing up that story? Oh, have you recently discovered you have a heart as well?"

Aariz did not respond. There was a fine line between being severed and illogical, but what was the point of explaining anything?

"Feroze, all I am saying is you don't believe in what you're doing. We have known each other for far too long to pretend otherwise."

"Aariz, tell me something. Are you jealous of what I am achieving in my life? Of who my father is?" Hashmatullah's voice came out from Feroze's vocal cords.

Aariz laughed sarcastically,"You really think I care about your father or what he-"

"Of course you do. Why wouldn't you? Unlike you, some people do get it all. And what do you know about fathers anyway? You are still ignorant of the idea despite having two of them. One died, and the other-"

"SHUT UP!" Aariz got up, outraged, ready to smack Feroze. But he stopped mid-way: if something had ended, there was no point in making a show of it. He looked at Feroze with bloodshot eyes, his heart pounding, pumping anger with every beat, and roared, "Fuck you, Feroze! Get out! Never show me your face again."

Feroze stood baffled for a while, then left without a word; in his shiny new car that had gathered smut in these hours.

The age of a friendship: eleven years.
The age of innocence: gone.

* * *

The end of one thing.
The beginning of another.

* * *

123

Bina and Mehar met for the first time in the dissection hall of the Anatomy Department. They both had come to the medical college in Lahore; one despite her family's wishes, one because of them.

While a group of students launched themselves on the dead body in the dissection room as if it was a Turkish delight, Mehar stayed back. She was in no mood to stuff her nose with the stench of formalin.

"And there's Sartorius. Now go towards its insertion. There, on the medial aspect of the shaft of the tibia. Near the tubercle. Yes, almost there."

Bina left the group and took a break from the proceedings, muttering something to herself, "There's no peace in death as well. Imagine a group of nerds pounding you when you're gone."

Mehar, the only other person standing there, looked at her and chuckled. Bina caught her eye and continued, "And imagine, I have to die multiple times."

Mehar played along, even though she did not understand what Bina meant.

"Can I have some water, please?" Bina asked.

Mehar handed her the bottle she was holding, and Bina kept talking.

"I came to the college promising myself that I'll find a rich husband out of this place and leave studies if I find them challenging. But look at what life has gifted me," she pointed towards the boys. "Now I will have to study!"

Mehar kept on laughing. Bina had a carefree, easygoing air about her that Mehar, who did not easily open up to people, couldn't help being drawn towards.

"I am only here to cut the bodies up and imagine them to be people I know," Mehar said after a while. Bina looked at her, surprised at the production of such dark words from a seemingly innocent face.

"Wow, you look too good for that."

"Don't we all?"

This was the first of the many meetings between them. Soon afterwards, they became close, opening their lives to each other, revealing the wounds the skin duly sheathed.

When Bina revealed all her family details to Mehar, right from the time when her father became a guest in his own house and down to the life Bina herself had experienced, plugged with its idiosyncrasies; she was pleasantly taken aback to see that Mehar took it as if there was nothing special there. It was, welcomingly, heartless: no consolation on being the child of a lesser god, no questions on the peculiarities of her beliefs, no interest in the degree of oppression her people faced. Bina understood that many in the country did this out of good intention - even if some had their own motives - but the equations built on this notion were transactions for her, not friendships. People often inflated Bina's defining features in contrast to the identity of the person herself, and Mehar was a refreshing exception to the rule. Mehar did not as much as hint that the difference of region, religion, ethnicity, or language was even remotely consequential for her.

She just saw Bina as who she was; the qualifications disappeared into thin air.

For them, college became, foremostly, the place where they had each other. Mehar commuted daily from her home, and Bina stayed in the hostel. Mehar never invited Bina to her house, even though her parents had shifted with Asad *bhai* to Rawalpindi, but would often stay in Bina's room in the hostel. The two girls would watch movies (Mehar had no specific choice, but Bina liked action), share poetry (Mehar would share the classics, Bina would only remember the verses written on the back of trucks), tell jokes (that no one else would find funny), shares notes of histology lectures (Mehar did it effortlessly, Bina waged war against the ideas) and discuss boys of the class (only Bina, Mehar would usually doze off by this point).

Bina knew better than to broach the topic of family with

Mehar. Even before Mehar delved into details about how trapped she felt in a Walled City amidst strangers she shared her blood with, Bina read into the reality that even if not religious, Mehar belonged to a minority in her own right.

One day, six months into their friendship, Bina came rushing to Mehar,

"Mehar, Papa called to tell me a proposal has come for me from Hyderabad."

"A marriage proposal?"

"Yes, those are the only proposals of interest to me."

"What does the boy do?"

"He said he's into business. But that is what all Hindu boys from Hyderabad think they do."

"So, what did you say?"

"I would have said yes right away. But there's only a small problem."

"Is the problem really that small? Will surgery help?" With Bina, Mehar found her sense of humour.

"Very funny. It's that the Hindu Marriage Act is not passed in Sindh. So if I kill my husband for his money, chances are I won't get any of it."

"If you kill your husband for money, I'll spray kerosene on you to burn you with him; and maybe prove that I was married to him." For a moment, Mehar forgot that she was already married.

That was what their friendship was to them. The laughter and respite helped both to forget the ruthlessness of the vast world outside the corridors of the place.

Mehar only stayed in medical college for about three years; she left only after cementing some timelines.

The age of a friendship: eternity.

The age of forgetfulness: temporary

Chapter Seventeen

IT HAD been raining in Lahore for three days. The conference of dark clouds led to bolts of lightning sparking through the sky, lending the city a makeover. As the roads became puddles of putrid water and sewage flew onto the streets, news of disease outbreaks spread. Cholera, typhoid, and gastroenteritis—the usual suspects. The many underpasses of the city became the home of resting waters: half-drowned cars that wished they would be better off as boats, making the motorcyclists wait in long queues in the underpasses for the rain to thin out as the slippery ascent would provide an amusing spectacle to the onlookers. Some rooftops collapsed in the peripheries of the city. Some people died. But it was also a time of jubilation in Lahore, much like every other time is. Boys gathered at the crossroads, taking their shirts off and dancing in the rain. Houses swelled with the aroma of spiced fritters and black tea. People went to the malls, and to the cinemas, and to meet old friends. Lovers considered this fate being on their side to take some forbidden liberties. Working people thought about innovative ailments to call in sick at work. Many took to Instagram to post romantic Urdu poetry with pictures of the soaked city they had taken. The rain was different things for different people, each disconnected from what it held for another.

The electricity had been off for an hour, and when the grid was restored, Cafe Utopia lit up like a revelation.

Four people were sitting at a table across the hall.

Aariz was the first one to enter the cafe. He handed his car keys over to the valet, told the waiter he needed a table for four people, and took a seat after being granted one. His wait wasn't long; Bina and Mehar arrived together in a cab. Bina hugged Aariz, and Mehar smiled at him. The three people decided they would only order after Feroze arrived, which happened ten minutes later. Feroze entered, and took some time to absorb the reality of the scene. He lunged at Aariz and hugged him like you hug a person you thought had died. He then turned towards Bina, and opened and closed his mouth various times without the production of any words, his eyes gesticulating as if they were attached with strings to the back of his head. When he saw Bina, his body shook with the agony of desire; she had transformed into a woman who attracts a man as much as she intimidates him. Bina smiled, weirdly signalled her arms and pivoted her head on her shoulders. She couldn't help but notice the gauze of white hair that streaked his hair, and that he had gained quite some weight. Feroze and Mehar gave each other a polite nod. There could be nothing the four of them wanted more than to be here, at this place, with each other.

The heart wants what it wants.

Want is a strange thing.

They all stole glances at each other to accept that this was really happening. It had been only once they all had sat together in one place, and it was a long time ago. But now that they were all together again, any loss of time between these two instances seemed superfluous. It was like yesterday.

But yesterday could have been a century ago.

Time is a continuum.

For once, they thought they were experiencing deja vu, that they had been here before; nothing had changed for either of them, nothing had changed either of them. They were as liable to share jokes, reveal secrets, travel together and talk to each other as they used to do once.

History repeats itself.

And then it starts: the suppressed recollections, the ghosts of the past, the unsaid things that arise in the mind of every person regarding the rest.

Feroze looks at Mehar and is transported back to when Bina first introduced him to her. He had been somewhat cautious about this friendship; clearly, Mehar was no match for Bina. She came from a lower socio-economic class, belonged to a grungy place, and had too much baggage attached. But these were only excuses; for Feroze, no one was a match for Bina. And for a Mehar-that-had-nothing to give competition to Feroze-that-had-everything regarding Bina's attention, the idea was insane for Feroze.

* * *

"Bina, you could have made better friends." He had told Bina over the phone after returning to Sukkur from Lahore, it was the second month of her medical college.

"Better friends?" Bina answered.

What do you know about friendships?

"My father has many friends in Lahore. You can easily hang out with the important people in Lahore. Why are you doing this to yourself?"

"Feroze, don't start. Mehar is my best friend. And she is a great person. And since when do you think I have started gauging a person's worth materialistically?"

"You cannot say material things are not important. My father-"

"I disagree with what your father says. There are things a lot more important than money. And Mehar is someone I look up to. She just has this strength that is difficult to describe." *Which you clearly don't.*

"You don't understand what strength is, Bina."

"You don't understand anything, Feroze."

* * *

Today, Feroze might be convinced by what Bina had said. Mehar sits across from him as if she is beyond all ideas, of strength or otherwise. She is out here in this world that is not hers, but is claiming it nevertheless.

Mehar catches Feroze looking at her. She never had any opinion about him as a person; Bina's attachment to him was all there was for Mehar to know about him. But objectively, Mehar was apprehensive about the idea of him and Bina. But this changed when Feroze turned from an unerring, apathetic figure into a mere, pitiable human for her. It happened when he had called her some months ago.

* * *

"Mehar, how are you?" It was after the day Mehar had returned to the Old City.

"I am good, Feroze. You tell? Is it anything important?" It was the first time they were talking on the phone, making Mehar a little queasy.

"Please give me Bina's number. I need to talk to her."

"You need to talk to her?" Mehar repeated dreamily; clearly, much was happening in her own life that she could have done without carrying loads of others for that one instance only. *You need to talk to her after all your family has done to hers?*

"Please give me her number. I don't have it. She changed it. I know you would have it." Feroze kept on asking without waiting for Mehar's reply.

Mehar thought for a minute, and since her agility was already compromised, she agreed.

You're a sorrowful, pathetic person, Feroze.

Feroze's tone changed; Mehar could hear the relief on the phone.

"And Mehar, I am sorry for what happened with you."

Mehar got curious. Clearly, he did not know about the divorce. But did he know about what had happened before? Maybe Bina would have told him something.

"I am sorry about you, too," Mehar said in her head.

* * *

Mehar is brought back to reality by Bina asking her which soup she would prefer. Mehar looks at her and tells her she would go with Bina's choice. She largely trusted Bina's views, except for a few times.

* * *

"Mehar, I need to tell you something." Bina had returned from Sukkur; it was the first day of their third year in medical college. She was agitated. "Papa told me something he had never told me before. You know how I told you our lands were taken from us? Papa always said only that much. This time, he told me something I never knew. Do you know who occupied our property? It was Feroze's father, Mehar. He cheated Papa."

Mehar listened.

"And that is the reason Papa didn't like our friendship. He wanted Feroze and me to be apart because this was what had been done to us by them."

"Does Feroze know this?" Mehar asked.

"I don't know." And after a while, "But either way, it wasn't Feroze's fault, really. What do you think?"

Mehar thought only one thing: all of Bina's marbles failed when it came to Feroze. She stayed silent.

"I am angry at him, but for Sharda. She was my sister. I can never forgive him for his laxity when she was kidnapped. But this is something that Feroze's father is to be blamed for."

Mehar gave her implicit agreement for whatever Bina was saying. Clearly, Bina did not want her opinion, only her ear.

And then she asked, "You really don't want anything to do with Feroze ever?"

Bina shook, surprised, and thoughtfully, "I don't know, Mehar. I don't know."

* * *

The waiter advances towards the group and waits for them to give him the order, but every person in that group takes a lot of time. Aariz puts his hand on Feroze's shoulder and says something sociable about his father. You have to remember dead people nicely; that's a rule. Feroze grabs Aariz's hand, like he had done some years ago.

* * *

Feroze was going to Sukkur for winter vacation in the ninth grade, and Aariz had, after all, convinced him that he needed to tell his father that politics was not for him. In the beginning, Feroze was unwelcoming towards the idea, but incessant convincing by Aariz had given him some strength.

"Don't tell him you want to be a cricketer. Just tell him you don't want to enter politics. That is the first step."

"But Aariz, he will be incensed."

"You will be devastated in your life Feroze if you don't work on what you want. Your father will understand, like fathers do."

But when Feroze finally said this to his father three days later, his father did not understand, like fathers don't.

Hashmatullah had stared blankly at Feroze for a while. He then lowered his head to his lap, brushing his eyebrows with his fingers.

Feroze was spooked out. He stood still.

And then Hashmatullah had said, "My shoulders have started

giving away. My body is turning old. And after all I have done in my life for my son, he comes here telling me that he will destroy all my ideals for him. I wish God had taken me away before showing me this day. Go, my son, do whatever you want; just don't give me a shoulder when I am taken to the grave."

Feroze had quavered with shame. He had failed his father; there could not be anything worse. He leapt at the feet of his father and cried. "Father, forgive me. I will never repeat anything like this. I am so sorry. Please forgive me."

When Feroze told Aariz this after returning from vacation, Aariz was taken aback by how conveniently Hashmatullah's law worked for him. But he didn't say this to Feroze; he only hugged him empathetically.

* * *

The waiter interrupts them, asking if they have decided what to order. They have, except for Bina, who is now asking how much salt there is exactly in a Singaporean soup. Mehar nudges her, and okays the order from her side.

* * *

Six years ago, Bina had asked Mehar, "Are you okay, Mehru?". It was the first time Mehar and Bina met after the former's marriage. Bina had to devise a specific strategy to materialise the meeting.

Mehar was silent. But clearly, she wasn't okay.

"Do you believe in ghosts, Bina?" She said.

"What?" This wasn't what Bina was expecting. She wanted Mehar to tell her details about her marriage, something she could soothe her friend with.

"You know, the people in my neighbourhood always said my father was possessed by ghosts; that was their only way to explain his behaviour. As a child, I thought it must have been the ghost of

Satnam Singh, who owned this house before 1947. He was angry at my father for occupying his home, so he possessed him."

Bina quivered uneasily, "Mehar, does your husband treat you well?"

Mehar looked at her and only smiled. Bina understood.

"Mehar, I will get you out of it. Don't worry. I will help you."

Mehar replied after a while, smiling, "No one gets as much help as they need, Bina."

***

Bina shifts in her chair and topples a bottle of water, spilling the liquid on the table. Mehar reaches for the tissue box. Aariz passes it over to Mehar, lying a little distance from her hand's reach. Mehar takes two tissues out of the box.

"What are you specialising in, Bina?" Feroze asks.

"Bones." She doesn't say orthopaedics, and giggles at Aariz, who is smiling at her already. Feroze looks at them and temporarily feels an indignant pang in his gut. His friends had bypassed him and become each other's confidants. He doesn't realise that eleven years is quite some period to engender and destroy bonds. He also doesn't know that Aariz had helped Bina decide to choose her training speciality.

***

"Do you really want to do this, Bina?" They were meeting after the completion of Bina's house job. "Do you really want to shift to Islamabad, and take up this field?"

"Yes, Aariz, but I wanted your opinion as well."

"Depends on your interest, but you can have your training in Lahore as well."

"But Islamabad will give me more exposure."

And it's a world away from Sukkur.

"Is that it?"

"Yes, and Islamabad is the activist pothole of the country. There is so much there that I cannot do elsewhere. Living in the capital puts you at the heart of what is happening in the country."

"Bina, can I ask you something?"

"Have you ever sought my permission before?"

"Do you want to correct everything else because the weight of that one thing you couldn't correct is too overbearing?"

Bina immediately looked at him, "Aariz, do you think that?"

"I think you are trying to make peace with the guilt you carry. You cannot heal the wound, so you do all possible to prevent an infection."

"Maybe, Aariz. I don't know. But isn't that just as well?"

"Maybe. But remember, it was not your fault. No one could have done anything. I just want you to always be sure that you have my unending support."

It was the first time Aariz had seen Bina teary-eyed.

* * *

"Something got into my eye," Feroze says as he wipes the water from his eyes with the back of his hand. Aariz offers him help. Someone turns the television on. A hotel staff member starts flicking the channels, and stops at a sports channel where a cricket match is going on.

* * *

"Where are we going, Aariz?" Some years ago, Feroze had come to meet Aariz at his invitation.

Though they did not go to the same educational institutions anymore, they still met at least twice a week.

"Happy Birthday, Feroze. Just a few years now before your back starts hurting. And you aren't even married yet. So best of luck with reproducing!"

Feroze hit him with his elbow and laughed, "I have enough stamina in me to populate a country."

And after a while, "But where are we going?"

"What is the date today? Besides your birthday?"

"Umm...."

"Pakistan plays Zimbabwe today in Gaddafi, dumb. Have you forgotten the return of International Cricket to Pakistan? We are going to watch the match, live. This is your birthday gift."

The pupils in Feroze's eyes dilated. He was at a loss for words. He wanted to thank Aariz, but he shrugged it off with a motion of his hand.

After they had watched the match, and Pakistan had won by 41 runs, and Feroze was in a state of exuberance and gratitude; Aariz took an alternate route back. He drove towards the home he had left; Feroze didn't ask him a thing as he understood. Aariz wanted to see his stepmother. He just tried to console himself with the idea that she was doing well. He didn't have anything against her particularly, but he had to detach himself from her as well.

Feroze only thought that you've got to do what you've got to do.

Aariz stopped the car in front of the park that his house lay across. They waited for half an hour, before she came out of the porch, Aariz's New Mama. She had come out to take the milk from the milkman. In the light of the gate lamp reflected on her face, Aariz was relieved to see that she seemed okay. That was all what he wanted to see.

He looked at Feroze, who smiled at him.

They held on to each other for a while, hugging.

* * *

The waiter brings them food. Feroze hands the rice to Bina, and she takes it with a grateful nod. Feroze's mind is spinning; he is already on to thinking about what he plans to say to Bina.

But not today, on another day.

Despite the mental races all their minds have bumbled upon, it's just a content affair for all of them. No one holds any grudges. No one brings up any points of friction, and no one says anything that would draw lines, close gates, activate the Gorgon, or detach someone. Everyone has forgiven everything, and tried their best to forget the rest.

It is as if the cosmos had designed it.

They sit for a long while, chat about many things, and laugh where laughing isn't only not required but is also reprehensible, and even the silence between them is comfortable - not laden with objections and justifications - but only a pleasurable nothingness. They talk in words that are comprehensible only to them, hands are slapped around, faces are made, and touches of laughter are crackled.

"Are we meeting again?" Feroze asks.

"All of us are in Lahore for a few days. We can meet again. But decide the place."

"I know an interesting place," Mehar says.

After a while, the lights in the cafe started buzzing; the voltage issues of the city a constant migraine for those who live here. As lights dimmed and flashed, all four of those people merged into the other. An onlooker would comment that he wouldn't be able to tell where one ended, and the other began. They were all one, as were their pilgrimages. It was like a single force, an entity espousing all of them. They were the same, and there was nothing to tell one apart from the other.

"He began the creation of man from clay, and made his progeny from a quintessence of fluid." God had already told everyone.

And then suddenly, the lights went out. Everything became the black hole of the cosmos.

"And He made you into nations and tribes...."

Chapter Eighteen

A MEMORY.

It was Mehar's thirteenth birthday. She came frolicking home, almost running, flaunting her result sheet by her side. She was a child of exceptional capabilities, decorously recognised by even those of her teachers who otherwise shied away from complimenting a pupil. She was fearless, an unruly critter that would take on humans and reptiles alike. She was gifted; her photographic memory often put her teachers in disarray: had she been cheating? She did not take kindly to authority and was reluctant to subscribe to society's rules of propriety, especially for a girl. She had topped in her class and was rushing toward home to garner a double birthday treat from her parents and her eldest brother, Asad. Along the way, she passed some jovial comments at random people: the man who sold overpriced locks and sneered at the gullibility of people, the uncle who made potato cutlets mixed with his bodily fluids, the cranky old man whose paunch increased every day and who'd always be reading a newspaper. And the boys of the muhalla: Toor, Hadi, and Hussain - all of whom she had beaten at one point or another. She entered her house, thrusting open the old wooden door, and after flinging her bag at a corner of the lobby downstairs, ran up the stairs where her parents would be.

She was about to fervidly call them when she heard a heated debate from inside a room. She stopped, listening.

"This girl is trouble. I have always told you that. The sooner she goes out of this house, the better." *Abba* was saying.

"Relax. Let me get you a glass of water." Amma replied.

"Take the water up your behind. I am telling you I am accepting the proposal. She's thirteen already, a good age for girls to be married off."

"She's just a kid."

"She's already more adult than all her brothers combined. This girl will disgrace us, I'm telling you. She hangs out with boys all the time. Has no aptitude for home-making. And defies all the rules of conduct. You want me to kill myself one day due to shame?"

"She's just different. She'll mature as she grows up."

"I don't want her to grow up in this house. And look at you, telling me what to do when you gave me a girl instead of a boy! I have to get rid of this menace."

"What does the boy do?"

"He would be fucking himself for all I care. I have already made two mistakes: one of not killing this girl when you cursed me with it, and the second of not selling her when I had the offer. If you try to do anything now, you and your daughter can bloody well get out of this house. Go prostitute yourselves with every man you find inside Delhi Gate. Your daughter will enjoy it anyway. So will you!"

There were some faint cries, some from inside and some from outside the room. Mehar's grip on the result card loosened, and it fell in front of the door. Later, when *Abba* left the room and Mehar had already gone out - contemplating to jump into the Dina Nath well - he stepped on it unknowingly. No one ever came to know about that result sheet in that house.

All the thirteen gates closed on Mehar-the-thirteen-year-old prostitute right then.

A MEMORY.

Mama re-married as soon as her *iddat* ended: the Islamic mourning period for a married woman.

Aariz had a new papa now. He remained aloof throughout the wedding festivities, albeit it was a low-profile event. On the night when the new papa came home, Aariz, for the first time, missed his real mother and old papa. Old papa had been so kind that Aariz had never really thought about his birth mother; old papa was the world for him. The new papa was also kind, he gave Aariz money and kissed him adoringly, calling him, "my son, my son!"

That night, Aariz, who was now ten but had shifted to his separate room at the age of eight, woke up shivering in the middle of the night. He ran to mama's room, but the door was locked, unlike before. He stood there for a while, waiting for mama to unlock the door. But the sound he heard was not of a bolt unlocking but far more complicated. It was something Aariz hadn't heard before.

The sound of flesh upon flesh.

Creaks and cries.

Was he hitting her?

Was she hitting him?

"Disgusting."

Aariz, eyes droopy with sleep, sat there and before he knew it, was out of his senses.

Six hours later, the door opened. Aariz's eyes opened with the shock of hitting the ground now that the door that supported his head was gone.

He saw him. New papa. He was shirtless, sporting a cloth below his navel that ended upwards of his knees.

"Look who we have here." He said in the kindest voice as he lifted the child in his arms.

"Unccle…" Aariz started, still getting back fully to his senses.

"Not uncle, dad."

"Mama?"

"She's in the washroom. Let's take this little champion to his room then."

And so he did. He carried Aariz all the way to his room, tucked him in the bed, talked to him in gibberish that Aariz found comic, and sat beside him. He kissed him on the forehead, and took his hands in his own. He held them for a while, and then squeezed them.

"Look at those delicate little hands. We'll toughen up our boy, won't we?"

Aariz was sleepy.

One hand of a naked adult male body ascended in the air and touched the little boys lips.

"And look at these petals."

Then, the kid saw a body approaching him to the extent of blinding him, so close that he could smell it: sweat and must.

"Disgusting."

A hand with veins protruding entered the blanket and discovered a little body, falling to places where that body wasn't used to having others' hands.

He froze.

He couldn't make sense of what was happening.

Soon enough, he would stop making sense of anything that happened.

A MEMORY.

"Bina, come," motioned Feroze, bellowing at Bina to sit in his car.

"Feroze, papa will scold me. He told me not to hang out with you."

"Oh, shut up, you scaredy cat. Get in!"

And Bina did. Like always.

For Feroze, she'd be okay with getting rebuked every single day. All her life.

They sat in the car, and the driver took the kids to where he knew he was to take them.

The Lansdowne Bridge.

They would sit at the bank of the river, throwing stones in the mighty Indus (Feroze would always win, but sometimes he would let Bina win too), while the driver, Abdul Shakoor, stood at a safe distance watching over the kids.

"I hate school," Bina said.

"I like mine," said Feroze. "It's this old, big school in Lahore, which the white people built and used to study in."

"Does it have date trees?"

"No, I haven't seen those in Lahore."

"Then here is better. I just hate the school."

Then they reverted to what they did best while here. Looking at the cars scurrying past them and blurting out notes on what they thought a car was destined towards.

"Look at that red car. It's going to a wedding."

"I think the person in that old, white car must be a druggie."

"Bet you that car is driving itself. They have magic cars in Amreeka now."

"Haha. Dumb. That truck is going to catch fairies in Saif-ul-Malook."

"That military vehicle is going to liberate Kashmir."

"The car which just took over the Mercedes must be going to its mom's wedding."

They laughed.

They always did, at the silliest of things.

Just as they were about to leave, they were greeted by a group of other kids. Two were Feroze's family friends. They rarely met because they had chosen the school in Bahawalpur, but they were still friends.

"Hey, Feroze," said one.

He replied.

After exchanging some pleasantries that kids so eagerly learn from their elders, one of the boy's eyes shifted towards Bina.

"Feroze, who's your friend… Isn't she Vankwani's daughter? The guy who works for your father?"

"With my father…"

"Look at you here," the boy turned rancid, "Hanging out with the scum from the lower caste, this Hindu girl; what would your father say?"

What would his father say?

Would he be disappointed? The thought shook him.

"Listen, you! Hang out with people from your own kind. Leave us alone. Feroze, mind yourself! You make us hang our heads in shame. These Hindus, you know how sly they are. Leave them with their million gods. Fucking *kaafirs.*"

Infidels.

Bina was silent.

"You know that line there, the border? You were supposed to be born on the other side of it. You don't belong here."

The line.

Some years ago, it was drawn across a region.

That day, it was drawn across a child's heart.

On the way back, Feroze was silent.

What would father say?

Bina did not say a thing. But when the kids drank water, she noticed that Feroze had, for the first time, refused to share his bottle of water with her, and handed her a separate one.

The line got darker.

A MEMORY.

Feroze had come back from his cricketing practice. He had become something of a marvel in his local school at the sport, and he used to go to practice with his friends whenever he had time. He would spend hours imitating Inzamam's batting style, could very well pull off a Wasim Akram, and would keep on perfecting what he called his Saeed Anwar spin. The only thing he was passionate about in life was cricket. He had collected posters of all his favourite cricketers, had bartered for postcards listing one-day international scores by exchanging his lunchbox with his classmates, and had sometimes ripped off the pages of the calendars published by the Pakistan Cricket Board that presented minute details of twelve cricketers: right from their dates of birth to their number of matches, runs and wickets, and pasted these on the walls of him room. He would take the sport up professionally, he was sure.

That day, father was not in his study.

Feroze was in his room when he heard a spat from downstairs. His parents were arguing over something. He ignored it and went to the bathroom to do what he loved to do: becoming his father.

He took a handful of shoe polish and splattered his across his face.

Baba's moustache.

Baba's beard that thinned out at the edges.

He had already perfected what he called his dad walk.

Just then, Baba entered his room. He didn't usually come there, but that day he did. Seeing Feroze in a comical presentation, he became livid and slapped him across the face.

"I wanted a prodigy, and all I have is a clown."

Feroze cried. Not because of the pain, but for disappointing his Baba.

Before leaving, Hashmatullah ran his eye around the room. Moin Khan, Yusuf Yohanna, Ramiz Raja looked back at him. He maintained the same look of derision for them he had given his son.

Later, Hashmatullah called Feroze in the lounge below. Feroze went, tiptoeing, afraid not to startle his father.

"Feroze," Baba said. "See what I have built for you. It was not easy."

"Yes, baba."

"You are my only son. And all you do is play cricket and hang out with your friends. Had I done what you are doing, you'd be rotting in a hellhole in this country like a piece of turd. Like millions of others. Would you have liked that?"

"No, baba."

"Then get serious in life. You are the one to carry this legacy forward. And no time is early enough to learn it."

"Yes, baba."

"I am sending you to a boarding school in Lahore, where they'll make a man of you."

Just then, Feroze noticed that Baba was sitting right across from the Gorgon. Feroze met its eye.

Stone.

Silence.

"You need to dedicate yourself to your studies, before you take on what I have built."

Silence.

"Oh, and for God's sake, no more cricket for you. Never again! Grow up."

A red coloured ball covered in white tape assumed the speed of 220 kph and hit the wicket, crushing all three stumps into dust.

"Shabbaraat, go to Feroze's room and remove all that cricket rubbish hanging in the room. Throw all of that away!"

There could have been tears. There could have been imploring.

But mercifully, there was only silence. And it was there to stay.

Chapter Nineteen

SOME DISTANCE from the Lahore metro's Shalimar Gardens station, an unassuming lane turns perpendicularly into another. On either side of the lane, carts and vendors suffocate the already narrow passage that sees a fateful competition between man and machine during all times of the day. The kids cajole their fathers into buying them potato chips off a cart, their mothers busy finding the cheapest deal on the glimmering shoes in the adjoining shops. The hawkers call for the fantastic discounts they are offering. One kilogram of onions for 20 rupees, not 40; coriander free. Every now and then, someone bumps into another. There's haste, laughter, and abuse. In Baghbanpura, one lane stands apart in this maze of flabby houses and a bluster of noises. About mid-way down this lane, on the right, a gate welcomes you to the shrine of Shah Hussain. Four people meet in that shrine that day. Two men, two women.

They are awkward at first. It is as if they are meeting for the first time, but they are not. They have been meeting each other for a long time. They had most likely met before assuming their current forms, somewhere in the skies.

A fire burns outside the shrine. People throw in candles and money. They plead and make offers, bargaining with divinity.

Everyone has something to ask for.

All of a sudden, a *dervish* springs to life. He throws his matted hair around in all directions, glistening with a coat of mustard oil, and stomps his feet on the ground as his amulets scream. He twirls, and swivels. People gather around him and take their phones out to record the dance.

Some give him money. He accepts, putting his hand on their heads before resuming his routine.

Inside, people pray to the grave of the holy man. They bow before him and supplicate. A newlywed bride enters the compound with her husband, and probably her new family, the redness of her dress inconspicuous among the barrage of colours already in the place. The visit is a note of gratitude. The bride's nuptials have been cemented owing to the baba's blessings.

Everyone has something to ask for.

Only some prayers are answered.

The four people jumble in a clumsy group near the graveyard, facing the grave of Ustaad Daman. One of the women recalls a specific verse the dead poet had written in a time when he hadn't yet become a dead poet:

"Ek dil tay lakh samjhavan waalay,

Kujj samajh naa aavay tay ki kariye?"

One heart, and so many to make it understand,

What do I do if I can understand nothing?

The living inhabit the place of the dead; the graveyard is full of people engaging in all sorts of activities that the world outside has shunned them for. Only among the dead have they found refuge, the souls of the departed keeping them safe company. Most of the men in the place are dressed in peculiar clothes, wearing silver jewellery interspersed with tags of wool, and they carry little bags with them that are their worlds - containing the instruments that are their means of escape from the real world. An old man, whose face is hidden due to the facial hair that hasn't met a blade in years, sitting at the corner of the graveyard, starts reciting verses from Hussain's poetry. His sidekicks join him in adorning the vocals with their harmoniums.

"Travellers, I, too, have to go
To the place of my beloved.
Is there anyone who will go with me?
I have begged many to accompany me,
And now I set out alone..."
Then there is ice-breaking.

"This *mela* was traditionally held inside the Shalimar Bagh," says the taller woman. "However, after partition, when Ajmer Sharif and Nizam Dargah were left on the other side of the border, someone had to rise to fill in the void of mysticism in Lahore, and it was decided that Data Darbaar should be regarded as the epitome of spirituality in Lahore. Shah Hussain took on the name of his Hindu disciple, Madho Lal, to immortalise their friendship, and such an act of defiance wasn't considered fit for a country having been born on the idea of difference."

She caught the attention of two people.

"Some say they are buried together here. What exactly was the relationship between them?" asked the other woman.

"That is for historians to answer." interrupted one man.

"Or lovers." said the other.

"During long nights, I have been tortured by my raw wounds.
Humble beggar Hussain says:
Oh God, send me a message..."
The family of the bride comes and offers them sweets. They accept bits of it.

For a while, everything is still, almost calm.

These four people could be taken as infallible friends, denuded of the baggage of the past and present they all carried. Shah Hussain wanted a world like that. They secretly did, too.

The sound of the *dhol* spears through the environs.

The smell of burning hashish flares their nostrils.

They talk in half sentences that make half sense.

Half questions.

Half answers.

Full prayers.

Suddenly, the calm is interrupted. Two policemen, otherwise privy and party to the open secrets of the place, are heard hounding a young couple at the side of the shrine. They are saying something about drugs and sex.

And right then, it happens.

The group of four people assumes focus.

Two men ask two women to marry them.

Everyone has something to ask for.

Only some prayers are answered.

Only one proposal is accepted.

Chapter Twenty

BINA IMMEDIATELY stormed out of the shrine when Feroze had asked her for marriage the night before. She was livid. What was he thinking? Why could he not understand?

He was an overgrown baby who had remained so much in his father's shadow that it was tough to make him understand anything. Bina was exasperated with the person he had become, the heartless, selfish prick he had monstrously transformed into. His eyes now reeked of complacency, his temperament always an air of being something. Meeting him after eleven years, Bina had been convinced that the Feroze she had homed in her mind was long gone. There was nothing common between them anymore; they came from two different dimensions of reality. Bina wanted to shake Feroze off and hammer his head against a wall to give him some sense.

Nothing makes sense, Aariz would say.

Will he scream? Mehar would ask.

At that point in their lives, all Bina wanted to do was to make peace with the past and start afresh. She was capable of doing that; she only needed closure with Feroze. To just be cordial with him, relishing their numerous memories but not letting them influence their future. She wanted to feel nothing for him. Not even anger.

Want is a strange thing.

Did Bina really want closure with Feroze? Or did she only

like the idea of it? What is closure anyway? In the world she came from, where the life of an individual was affected by so much that was out of their control, where dead people haunted the living, and the living shaped the dead, where history and legacy became a character of their own in the living world, where lines and struggles enjoyed an immense power of decision independently, wasn't closure a very fanciful ideal? Or did she desire it only because she had convinced herself it was the only practical way forward? The only realistic exit from the maze they were in?

That's your line.

This is my line.

We can wave at each other but not cross these.

But then, it was Feroze. What Bina wanted, and what she desired, and what she expected, and what she feared, were all separate things.

Everything is so complicated, thought the practical Bina.

She texted Feroze. She had to do this.

"Dinner at 8? You decide the place."

* * *

After their meeting at Shah Hussain, Feroze returned to the government rest house he was staying in. He had left the place after Bina did, calling her, shouting her name, but she had disappeared in the madding crowd like she had disappeared from his life years ago and from Sukkur.

Bina knew something about disappearing.

While coming to his room, Feroze drove beside the Canal that ran through Lahore, poplar trees fencing the receding water level from foul attention. His Prado ran along the murky waters that separated the road, and the city. The traffic police personnel deputed at the crossroads bowed obediently towards Feroze's car as it ran past them, owing to its official number plate, before hurrying to fine a motorcyclist without a helmet. In many places, families crowded the Canal; the kids jumped into the water, and the elders munched on fruit as they sat looking. The girls only entered the water where the traffic was less; the boys displayed all the swimming skills they had taught themselves, the half-breast stroke, the uncanny freestyle. Feroze was untouched by the spectacle. If anything, he found it repulsive.

How can people be happy?

What is there to be happy about?

Feroze received Bina's text in the evening, when his mind had already wandered to coming up with new ideas for meeting her. He was exhilirated at reading her words. He had feared Bina might not talk to him for another eleven years. The thought had killed him. He readied himself hurriedly; it was about an hour to 8 pm. He applied deodorant, put on his unironed black shirt (because Bina liked black) and sprayed two gusts of hairspray on his head. He hadn't shaved for two days, but the stubble suited him fine.

Maybe, she has changed her decision.

Maybe, their hearts wanted the same thing.

* * *

About an hour later, they sat in a Chinese restaurant in the Defence Housing Colony, which had dim, red lanterns and an oriental ambiance. On a wall hung a painting of the Cowherd and the Weaver Girl; Bina recognised it. A fairy and a cowherd fell in love once, but Chinese folklore has always been clear about the rules of conduct. A celestial figure and a mortal being ending up together was against the rules, and those who tamper with these in Chinese mythology are often separated as a punishment. The goddess got angry with this unruly behaviour, and scratched a river in the sky. The river became the Milky Way. The man and woman became the two stars on either side of it. The weaver girl now sits on one end of the river and the cowherd on the other; they can look at each other with longing, but cannot cross the line.

"Rules are rules. If you try changing them, they'll destroy you," Hashmatullah had said.

Bina looked around, the waiters were all Pakistani, but the receptionist was a Chinese man in his mid-forties. Bina took some time examining the menu and ordered for both of them. Feroze thought he had already received what he had asked for.

Even though Feroze wasn't the one to be initiating conversations, he started, "Bina, I got to know what my father did, I assure you…" Even if he had denounced the silence, he still couldn't say the word "cheat"; Bina interrupted him mid-way.

"Feroze, listen-"

"I will return everything, don't you worry-"

"Feroze, listen to me."

* * *

"Feroze, listen to me!" a twelve-year-old Bina shouted at Feroze.

He had already run into the fields before her, catching earthworms. They had a competition for who would catch more. They would then collect their finds and leave them as a gift beneath a date tree, whose lucky day it was, because Bina had learned in school that they aerated the soil for the plants.

"Come, Bina, you'll lose it."

"Feroze," Bina shouted again, "listen to me. Come here."

Feroze stopped, and made his way toward Bina.

"What is it, Beeeena?"

"Feroze, Papa says we shouldn't meet. He says he'll send me to Karachi if we keep meeting."

"Why? What is his problem, Bina?"

"He just says we are different. That we will realise it when we get older. That he and your father were friends as well, but then something happened. Likewise, something will happen to us."

"No, Bina. Don't listen to him. Nothing will happen to us. Everything will be fine one day. When we grow up, we will have a kingdom of our own. You and me. We'll rule together, and play cricket and make a great stadium, and will have many animals around, and we will build temples and mosques, and we will give free food to the people. Everyone will look at our kingdom and get jealous of us."

Bina smiled. She liked the idea. There was one problem, though.

"But we don't have any land, Feroze. Papa says all his land was taken from him."

"All of my lands will be yours, Bina. In fact, all the land everywhere will belong to everyone in our kingdom."

"Okay," Bina was convinced. "And we'll buy cars. I'll get one in red colour. I'll always decorate it the way they do at weddings. A lot of white roses and petunias."

"Okay, and Shahid Afridi and Saeed Anwar will also come to live with us in our kingdom. They'll be my best friends." And after a while, "After you, of course."

Suddenly, Bina was concerned, "But your father will not let you do all this, Feroze. He'll make you do what he does. Meeting people and giving speeches."

"No, Bina. My father will agree to everything I say. He loves me very much. I'll ask him for one kingdom, and he will give me two."

"Okay," and then, thoughtfully, "And Feroze, can we plant many date trees in our kingdom?"

"There are so many date trees here already. But we can have more if you say so."

"Great! And will it have a big throne for me to sit upon?"

"It will, definitely."

"It will be so much fun, Feroze. *Mukhaan ta intizaar natho thye wado thyanr jo.*"

I cannot wait to grow up.

"And I will also have a big swimming pool in the kingdom. We will keep the Indus dolphins in it."

This was the only part of the idea that Bina did not like.

* * *

Feroze was startled back to reality. The Chinese man at the counter was looking at him. How long had they been sitting there? Bina had asked him to listen to her; what had happened afterwards? A crack appeared on his brow. This was not the routine starting line of an acceptance speech.

"You have everything one could ask for, Feroze." Bina was saying. "Money, power, status. Soon enough, you'll also find a person to share these with you. But that person is not me."

Suddenly, it was cold in the restaurant.

"What's in the past is in the past. Let's not ruin that. But we have come a long way since. There are some ideas that sound pretty only as ideas. They have no practical connotations whatsoever. I hope we are mature enough to understand that."

The food arrived. No one ate it.

"I would like us to always be friends. We have practically spent our childhoods together. But that is all that we can be."

A glass dropped at the other table, bursting into a thousand little pieces that would never be joined.

"I have to tell you something, Feroze. I am getting married next month. You have to come, for sure. You will come, right? You'll like meeting Abhimanyu; he's a fine person."

Bina looked at Feroze's eyes as she said this. But Feroze found in Bina's eyes the sight of the Gorgon.

Stone.

Silence.

* * *

Two minutes later, the waiter serving the food at table number four noticed the woman leaving the hotel without eating anything.

These privileged people and how they waste food, he thought. He observed the woman rushing out of the door with derision. But was she crying? He looked back at the table and saw the man sobbing silently, looking at his feet to avoid public attention.

"This is not practical." Bina had said.

But the heart wants what it wants.

Want is a strange thing.

Chapter Twenty One

THE HOURS of load-shedding were consistently being increased in the country. It was as much a social woe as a political one: every party that came to power avowed it would end the power crisis before coming to power but would put the burden of responsibility on the previous party after assuming the parliament. And the usual drill was put on repeat telecast: building dams, controlling population, cheap imports. This was a dance happening for as long as Mehar could remember. She had read reports about the country missing its Polio eradication goal because the vaccine couldn't be refrigerated, or the economy going through a steep slide as the industries did not have electricity to run their plants. This was the usual; like so many other things, the people had become used to this as well; those who could afford them had installed generators in their houses, relied on Uninterruptible Power Supply, or invested in solar panels; but for the majority, the worst came in August in Lahore. With monsoons at the helm, the humidity copulated with the heat and blocked the airways, impeding the airflow to the lungs and collapsing the little sacs in the lungs that transported oxygen to the body.

It became suffocating, both inside and outside.

But humans have this inexplicable capacity for resilience. Like cockroaches, they will survive just about anything.

Like Mehar.

Mehar tied the curtains neatly and turned on the pedestal fan on the balcony. No one was playing the radio that day; all she could hear was the prankish laughter of the children running in the street below. They probably had again messed with a shopkeeper, taken some edibles away, abused someone's mother, and ran off. So much had happened in a day, and she hadn't had the time to process it.

She had agreed to marry Aariz; she wouldn't explain the reasons to anyone. It perhaps was about getting out of here, but there was much more to it.

He was so complicated for her. A man who could be gentle and nice, whose greatest achievement in life wasn't flexing a biological gift; a man who was also a riddle. Who lived within his maze of incredulous ideas and exceptional vision. Unlike the men she had known all her life.

If you know one, you know them all.

She knew Aariz and she were on to something for a while. She knew this would lead here, she wanted this to lead here, but she had never considered the exact dynamics of how it would unroll. She did not question the dynamics of this relationship, and Aariz's choice to opt for her when he could have, ostensibly, fared better.

Because she now understood that the gates open and close to no one's orders.

Mehar searched for a cigarette, and was chafed to see she had none left. In the early days after returning to her house, she would get them delivered through the neighbour's boy, tipping him off for five rupees for every visit he made to the store. Now, she went herself. No one cared anymore; no one rolled their eyes; people did not talk to her. Even the women who had frequented her, in the beginning, to get some juice out of her as to how sexually oppressive her husband was had stopped talking to her in more than the customary greetings. She crossed her room to go downstairs and outside.

She thought it was because everyone thought she was vermin.

That engaging with her might reduce the standing of others. What proper person talks to a woman who has been divorced by her husband after being enjoyed by all his friends as well? She thought they might consider her a bad influence since she did not bear any children - the details of the abortion were something she had confided in only Bina - and who had helped her get through the process.

But Mehar did not know the sub-plot of this happening was something else. The reason was that in those houses, and shops, and lanes, people had started talking about her in low voices and were now referring to her as the *Laal Pari.*

The Red Fairy.

It started with Chacha Abdul Kareem and his dream. Chacha's family were all devotees of Lal Shahbaz Qalandar, and they used to go annually to his urs in Sehwan Sharif. Some people questioned this; they were from Lahore - *Data ki Nagri* - after all, and had other arenas of seeking blessings instead of going all the way to Southern Sindh.

"Data *sahab* stopped the Indian bombs from exploding in the 1965 war, and you will go all the way to the other end of the country to pray?" People had asked in the beginning.

But Chacha rarely heeded these objections. Because he knew that human reasoning was as limited as human understanding. The heart wants what it wants, and that is about it. Besides, visiting Sehwan ran in his family, and the tradition had been running long before the present shape of either Sindh or Punjab had taken form. There, at Lal Shahbaz Qalander's shrine, after the routine supplications and rituals, they would often seek out the Laal Pari, the arcane woman at the shrine who would always be dressed in red, and who, it was believed, had mystical powers. Laal Pari was always a vision: a valiant, commanding woman in a sea of men, demanding reverence and deification from all around her. She was a misfit who had claimed her space so ferociously that no one dared question it. Chacha's family would seek her blessings, and good things would happen to them. Chacha always claimed that his life had turned upside down since the Laal Pari had died. An era had ended. Nothing would ever be the same, and the first bitter realisation of this came when a suicide bomber attacked the shrine, killing eighty people. The country had been shackled by a round of religious extremism, and those seeking an ever-puritanical version of Islam thought that the heretic legacies of Sufis had no place in the Islamic Republic. Sehwan was not the only shrine attacked, but for Chacha's family, the attack on it was clearly the most unfortunate as it was the most personal. A few days after the attack, a leading kathak dancer of the country had gone to the recently attacked shrine and indulged in *dhamaal* in full public view.

Everything symbolises resistance when the going gets tough: dancing, smiling, breathing.

This had made news; the picture of the woman dancing in the shrine against all odds was hailed as something of a rightful mutiny.

Was the Laal Pari manifesting herself through her? Chacha had thought. This tragedy wasn't a cause of concern for only Chacha and his family; his family's visits to Sehwan Sharif were also considered blissful to all around him. They prayed for them all and blessed them, the Laal Pari.

And one day, months after Mehar had returned to her house in the Old City, Chacha had woken up in the middle of the night to announce to his wife: the Laal Pari had returned.

The news got out soon, partly because of Chacha's enthusiasm to spread it and its controversial nature. Scoop always surpassed the speed of light while travelling through Old Lahore. Everyone was first extremely cautious, almost apprehensive, about this claim that Laal Pari had come in Chacha's dream and told him that to seek her blessings, they would have to revere Mehar.

The slut?

Some neighbours first thought Chacha was finally giving in to dementia, like all people do after crossing a certain age. But so sure was Chacha about this claim, and such trust-worthy was his standing, that people soon started considering what he said. Chacha, after all, had a point, they persuaded themselves. And it wasn't long before everything Mehar did casually would be tagged as a sign, an action of some higher power.

"Look at her walking like she doesn't care, her feet barely touching the ground, and her gaze into the space; that's because she is in touch with another reality now."

"When she came to my shop that day to get vegetables, my business increased two-fold."

"As she smoked a cigarette that day, I saw from my room a strange figure emerge in the smoke."

"I have heard her husband has had some infection, and they had to cut his organ off."

"Beware of her curse; see how her brother and sister-in-law are still childless all because of mistreating her?"

At first, Mehar did not read much into the changed behaviour of the people towards her. She had never really cared. But it helped that no one was pushing anything down her throat anymore.

Sometimes, she would exploit it as well. As a neighbourhood aunt would proceed towards asking Mehar something she did not want to tell, she would just look into the questioning eyes without blinking, and that would do the trick.

Whether Chacha Abdul Kareem had actually seen Laal Pari in his dream or made the story up because he had always liked Mehar since she was a kid and felt sorry for her, only he can tell.

* * *

Aariz was coming to the Old City that day. The consultancy he was doing required him to plan on the potential of the widening of lanes in the area, the under-grounding of electric wires, the installation of beautification items, and the up-gradation of the sewerage lines. He had tagged along two of his interns with him,

161

freelancing. Mehar got ready to see him. Just a bit of kohl in her eyes, nothing else. Two streets down her house, Nashmia was getting ready to set up the already set couple. She would never miss an opportunity where she could sprinkle some hot pepper. She and Mehr were the same age, and Mehar knew if there was one person who could turn this meeting into something it was not supposed to be, it would be her.

Mehar went to Nashmia's house, where an already waiting Nashmia discarded her sense of fashion with an exasperated gaze (Are you going to a funeral? Where's the lipstick?). Mehar evaded the question by pointing out that Aariz would have arrived already. Their meeting point was just in front of the Sunehri Masjid, and the women left.

As the two women approached the group of men, one of the interns flashed his camera and took a picture. That was it; Mehar and Aariz did not have much time to engage in routine courtesies.

"Excuse me, who do you think you are?" Nashmia started. "Taking pictures of ladies as if we are your sisters. Don't they teach you manners in your fancy schools, where you're so well trained to shake your bodies? Call your sisters; my brothers want to take their pictures too."

Nashmia was the most inappropriate woman in Old Lahore.

Aariz started; Mehar stopped him with a smile.

Enjoy the show!

The intern responded, "No, sorry, I was just taking a picture of the building there."

"You *mummy daddy* type people come to our houses and start taking their pictures. Are there no houses in your DHA VHA? Hello, this is where we live. It is not an exhibition for you people. You write books about this place, and have your fancy picture exhibitions about it, but have no frigging idea about the life here. You get the 'feels' here, right? Isn't there a more elitist way to let out your superiority complex?"

Nashmia was the loudest woman in Old Lahore.

Aariz and Mehar had taken a side and were looking at the proceedings, amused.

"Madam, we are just trying to capture…."

"I know what you are trying to capture. Every half-bred man like you has only one thing in your mind when you come here. The *Heera Mandi*, right? That is all you romanticise about, the famous Red Light area, where you'll get to see your Umrao *Jaans* and wag your little tools."

Nashmia was the brashest woman in Old Lahore.

Mehar and Aariz secretly sniggered. The interns had turned red by then.

"No, madam, we are working to improve your neighbourhood…."

"Are we animals that need help from you *burger* people to better our homes? What are we to you, charity cases? Hello, we don't need charity; hit up an Edhi home. If our neighbourhood is so bad, why do all of you keep coming here in droves? Polluting these narrow lanes with your bulky existences? You like the area, right? Here's a deal. How about you exchange your house with mine? Then you can improve here all you want."

Nashmia was the vilest woman in Old Lahore.

After engaging in this banter that was sure to have lifted her spirits, Nashmia turned towards Mehar and Aariz, and whispered before shouting a "shoo" at the interns: "Listen, you two. Always helps to talk before marriage. Who is there to teach that to our society, *uff*? I have told my family that one of our distant relatives has died. They have all gone to Masti Gate, and since Papa has a bad leg, it will take them a while to realise my lie and return. You guys can go to my place. Meanwhile, I will help these pretty boys take some good pictures and feed them McDonald's," she winked.

She took a few steps and looked back to tell Aariz, "Oh, and there's no McDonalds in the Walled City."

Mehar laughed.

* * *

Aariz and Mehar left the Old City for a drive. They appreciated Nashmia's sly scheme to grant them privacy, Aariz was particularly entertained with it, but they let the offer pass since neither of them was looking for such privacy that invited the simple ritual that men and women had been naturally indulging in for times immemorial. Aariz offered to drive Mehar around the city; if he cared even slightly about the renovation, he didn't let it come in the way of the plan. Mehar agreed silently.

Soon, they were off into the parts of the city that Mehar had rarely been to. She thought she knew Lahore, but realised that day there was so much more to the city than she had been accustomed to. Mehar lit a cigarette while she observed how after every mile, the city would start taking a shape she couldn't recognise. Cities, like humans, were also composed of layers of unexplored treasures, and Mehar gazed with awe at Aariz's Lahore, which was a part of the same city yet so disjoined by it.

They passed by the billboards that displayed stage shows' timings with actresses clad in skimpy clothes, and wearing contact lenses of a greyish hue that gave them a supernatural disposition. They passed through numerous traffic signals that switched their colours and which people were eager to bypass after ensuring no traffic police personnel waited in the shadow in the distance. They passed through buildings that gave others competition as to which one stood taller and which one stood longer. They passed through electronic billboards shining in succession in the divider of some roads that told people how imperative it was for them to buy this soap, or those shoes. They passed through the underpasses, which became bridges, and then intersected the track of the public transportation. They passed through lavish designer stores that proudly displayed apparel that Mehar never thought she would ever be able to afford. The fumes transformed into oxygen, and the debris of a fallen building gave birth to an amaltas tree some miles ahead. And they passed through various people, some driving, some walking, becoming a part of their lives for one important minute and then continuing as if they had never met, to never remember that one time in one place, they had been together; almost one.

"We live in the same city, yet in two completely different worlds," Mehar said after a while.

"Which world do you like better?" Aariz asked.

"The world without gates."

"Gates?"

"Hmm."

Aariz looked at her, interested. Mehar signalled him to keep his eyes on the road.

"You don't speak a lot, do you?"

"I have nothing to say that the poets haven't said already."

"And what poets would those be? Mir, Ghalib, Faiz, Jalib? Those are all the Urdu poets I know."

"I read English and Punjabi too; I know it's hard to believe the former." Mehar gave Aariz a warm smile that took away any intent of objection in her words. Aariz abused himself under his breath. "So yes, I've read the names you gave. And a lot of others. Every second person is a poet in my part of the city. And every third person, a storyteller." Mehar said.

"And you don't share a lot as well! Have the storytellers shared all of that?" Aariz smiled, covering his faux pas with humour. Mehar did not hold anything against him.

"Words are only one way to share."

"And what are the other ways?"

"It will be ironic to use words for an idea that is independent of them." Aariz looked at her, taking in the wordiness of her statement, and smiled. She had a calm, unflinching expression.

"Bina always told me you were brilliant in medical college. She was always impressed by you."

"And she always said good things about you as well, Aariz. I initially thought she found a charity case in me; you know how

Bina is. I took some time to settle into the friendship. And I think she took some time to reconcile who I am and where I come from."

"Where you come from? What does that have to do with anything?" Aariz clearly knew what that meant, but he feigned ignorance.

"Class has to do with everything, Aariz. Somehow, intellect seems more fitting when it comes from money. I appreciate your kindness, but let's not pretend we don't know it." Aariz blushed slightly, guilty that he also hadn't expected much from Mehar initially. Even her ability to speak Urdu without a Punjabi accent was something he had found a bit odd in the beginning. The fact that she could speak English had taken him by surprise. She spoke the language immaculately, but their accents differed, much like their cities.

"But the Old City is enchanting." Aariz tried to steer the conversation to safer waters.

"It is. But that is one way to describe it."

Aariz picked a small jar of medicine from the dashboard of the car, and popped in a pill.

"What is that for?" Mehar asked.

"Headaches. My constant companion in life. Anyway, why do you hate the Old City so much?"

"I cannot hate it any more than I can hate myself. It's a part of me. But there are some parts of you that you like to pretend don't exist. Anyway, do you like your part of the city, Aariz?"

"I don't know if it's about the city or my little associations, but I am okay with it. When I left it, I thought I'd miss it - the store I used to go with Papa to, the park we used to play catch in, the dens Feroze and I used to sneak off to, the cafes Bina and I had interesting debates in; you know - the little things; but interestingly, I never missed it. I remembered it passively, and that is about it."

"Remembrance is never passive, Aariz. It's the war of memory against forgetting," Mehar said after listening to Aariz attentively.

"Mehar, do you think life was unjust to you?"

"Unjust?" Mehar looked at Aariz as if she wasn't expecting this from him. "Justice is an abstract idea, Aariz. The fact that we are roaming today in Lahore in your air-conditioned car while there are people in this country who quench their thirst out of sewers and boil leaves in water for a meal is inherently unjust." She took a break before resuming, "Life gives you pain, that is true. But the only person without pain is the person you haven't asked. And I try never to lose sight of the fact that many others' lives have caused them a lot more hurt than mine has."

Aariz looked at her again.

God created Adam from a handful that He took from all of the earth. So the children of Adam come by the earth they are created from; some of them come red, some white and black, some thin, some clean. Were Aariz and Mehar created from the same sample of clay?

"And Mehar, do you think the pain will go away if you leave the Old City?"

"I don't want the pain to go away. It will be turning my back on myself."

"You want the pain to stay?"

"I only want to be worthy of it."

"And what about those who inflicted this pain upon you?" Suddenly, Aariz thought about his stepfather.

"The inflicter of pain is a lot more pitiable than the inflicted," Mehar said, more to herself than Aariz, who had lightened his foot on the accelerator.

"Is it that easy, Mehar? Forgiveness?"

"Nothing is easy, Aariz. You think you are there, but then you fall back. Forgiveness is a process. You char your insides thinking about retribution, and brutal ways to get back at your inflicters before realising what you wanted was already granted. Their hell burns a lot hotter than yours."

"Their hell? But they might be leading normal lives. They might not be burning in hell at all." Aariz wasn't sure if he was talking to himself or to Mehar.

"That makes it all the worse for them. In psychiatry, we called it insight. It's when a person with a mental disorder doesn't even know he has a disorder. So his ability to improve things is also lost on him. Those who do not know they are in hell end up burning before realising they ought to get out."

Their car stopped at a signal, from which roads went in all directions. A masseuse interrupted their conversation by clinking the iron in his hands, a balloon seller called at them to buy the electric balloons he had recently added to his stock, and a woman rushed towards the car and directed her spray bottle at the windshield before Aariz shook his head, two transgenders in gaudy makeup advanced towards their car, praying to God to bless the beautiful couple with a son. The signal turned green.

"Are you happy, Mehar?"

Mehar smiled. "Happiness is a mirage, Aariz. It is not something you can achieve. But you keep trying, and it keeps you going."

"Are you saying the pursuit is happiness?" Aariz raised an eyebrow.

"The American constitution agrees." Mehar smiled.

"Do you read a lot?"

"I have a human library. It's called Bina."

Aariz laughed, "Yeah, one session with Bina is worth ten books."

"But seriously, yes, I read. There wasn't much to do in my life besides it. But I have read a lot less than you, Aariz. I used to read your articles too. Bina would get me the magazines as they wouldn't be available in my Lahore."

"Is that why you don't ask me any questions? Because you have read me?"

"No, it's because there always are many more questions than answers."

"Did you think I was outrageous, reading what I wrote?"

"No, I thought God was showing me so much I didn't know."

"Are you religious?"

"Sometimes I am, sometimes I am not. Are you, Aariz?"

Aariz stayed silent.

Mehar continued, "But I believe in the supreme power. I pray to Him regularly, half driven by faith, half by habit. And it's something that has been quite helpful to me."

"And do you think the supreme power listens to you?"

Mehar looked at Aariz and smiled, "He does."

Chapter Twenty Two

AS KIDS, Bina and Feroze would often go to the Sadhu Belo temple, primarily because they relished the boat ride to the island. It was cradled, alongside other structures, on a little island in the Indus - its picturesque outline being lauded by both the children as it came into their view. Inside, people would pray to Mother Annapurna for food; the nine temples of the complex would simmer with devotees and pilgrims, but the children's primary focus of interest during the trips was the river's dolphins. The blind dolphin of the Indus, Bhulan, was something they were always on the lookout for. They never saw one, owing to the scanty population of the same. Bina's uncle had told her that the dolphin was once a woman, cursed by a holy saint because she forgot to feed him one day, and he turned her into a blind dolphin: the state in which she has existed since then. Feroze did not believe this story. Bina did, but nudged it off owing to his disapproval; while deep inside, she feared that the day a dolphin came out of the water near Sadhu Belo would not be a good omen. It was only for this reason that Bina had always affected illness whenever Feroze had told her that one of his father's friends who worked in the Wildlife Department was calling them to be shown the Indus Dolphin. Why would she bring lousy luck upon herself? Afloat on the Indus with Feroze, though, she became a sport: she pretended to search for the dolphins with him while secretly praying they spotted none.

* * *

Bina and Abhimanyu entered the temple, their families by their sides. Bina was dressed in her mother's sari, dark pink with emblems in red at the sides. Mehar, who had arrived a day ago for the first time in Sukkur, held her friend's dress so that it did not sweep the floor. Aariz had just reached the venue; he would head back to Lahore as the ceremony ended, he had told Bina. Abhimanyu was wearing a bright, long kameez with a shalwar, a turban of *ajrak* tied neatly around his head. Bina looked around at the people, clandestinely trying to locate Feroze, but he hadn't come. She was mildly disgruntled, as if the credibility of this ritual would falter in its finality if Feroze were not a spectator to it.

Today was their *vivah;* it was designed by the cosmos.

A group of children on a wooden boat swivelling above the layers of the Indus, wearing only shalwars and revealing their slender, sunburnt upper bodies, shouted in unison outside the temple.

"There, there! Look!"

They have spotted Bhulan.

The cosmos works in peculiar ways.

* * *

Some miles away from the temple, a man sat visibly agitated in a room on the upper storey of an opulent mansion. He was obsessed; his existence had been reduced to shambles. He was still at a loss to process his feelings, or channel them in any sensible fashion.

He was a lost cause.

After taking everything in his life with silence, Feroze let it all out. He shouted, tossed around everything that came his way, punched the wall and contused his hand, and broke the dresser's mirror that entered his skin. He screamed, but that day there was no one in the house to attend to him.

Feroze thought about everything that had happened, what he had become, what had Bina and Feroze become? What was there to begin with? He bawled his eyes out, his heart sinking into the dreadful pool of tears.

He picked up a piece of the shattered mirror and looked at himself. His reflection looked back, independent.

Who exactly am I?

Today is the day Bina will become someone else's.

Forever.

There are things that you innately consider yourself immune to; some things are meant for others. Like death. Like the abduction of your sister. Like the estrangement of your beloved. You can read and empathise with them, but you slide past the need to prepare to deal with them. You are only supposed to live them vicariously.

What do you do when they happen to you?

He cried out louder.

He needed to talk to her.

But what was there to say?

What was surmountable and what was not?

He would ask for her forgiveness, tell her he was sorry for what happened and all he said and did, and seek her guidance for a way out. He would apologise as much for his silence as for his words. Indeed, there ought to be a way for repentance and for rectification? Whatever she says, he will agree with her. For the first time in his life, he would undo everything others thought was important for him and do only what he thought was essential.

It was time to surrender a dead father to his grave.

He was sure the plan would work.

"You are not sure, Feroze. You have never been sure. You were never allowed to learn how to be sure." What Aariz had said years ago came ringing back to Feroze.

Feroze shook the words off him, whipping them off his arms like they were maggots possessing him.

Why the hell is everything suspended in the air?

Despite being in infrequent contact with Bina all those years, he had known she was there. He had assumed she was waiting.

For what?

The lines to blur?

The cosmos laughed.

Feroze rambled around like an irate dog. He had become what he had never set out to be, but then it could be fixed. Every story comes with an intrinsic potential of being re-drafted.

What was defensible and what was not?

He searched for his phone to call Bina and say whatever he wanted to tell her.

But what was there to say?

That they should go back to Lansdowne bridge to make stories about cars?

That they should live as star-crossed lovers?

That they should let the cosmos decide?

* * *

The cosmos had decided.

The fire was lit. It would be a witness to their union.

Aarti, Bina's mother, stood by her side; tears dripped continuously from her eyes. "We will all go to Hinglaj together now," she whispered in Bina's ear, who hugged her mother at using the excuse of Hinglaj yet another time to pivot her sentiments. Shreeshanth Vankwani came forward and tied the end of her daughter's sari with Abhimanyu's turban - *kanyadaan*. Bina touched his feet, containing the tides of the ocean surfacing in her eyes. He planted a kiss on her forehead and then directed her toward her soon-to-be husband. Bina and Abhimanyu faced each other with the look reserved for those critical junctures in the transition between *what-was* and *what-will-be;* their expressions a shade of rustic calm.

After some moments, their lives would be intertwined forever;

encompassing the grand scheme of affairs to the network of lines on their palms.

The chants started, activity pursued.

Bina and Abhimanyu stood up to circle around the fire seven times.

In another room, another world, Feroze got his phone and dialled Bina's number. Mehar thought she felt a vibration from inside Bina's purse that she was clutching, but overlooked the probable and focused on throwing flowers at the couple and being happy for them.

The *pheras* - rounds - had started.

During the first call, Bina and Abhimanyu had promised each other to stay and go on pilgrimage as a couple. They had avowed their gratitude to divinity for food and water, and they prayed for strength to live together - packed with love and respect.

When Feroze called again, Bina and Abhimanyu had pledged to grow as one in physical, mental and spiritual strength, declaring equal respect for their parents.

During the third call, they pledged to earn an honourable livelihood and prayed for their wealth to be increased by virtuous means and for its meaningful utilisation.

As Feroze called for the fourth time, the couple had vowed to take on the responsibility of fulfilling the family's needs. They had declared their quest to pursue wisdom, happiness, and harmony by mutual love and trust and wished for a long, joyful life together.

The fifth call had the couple pray for children. They desired to have healthy and virtuous children, and Bina asked Abhimanyu for his alliance in running the house and to invest his time in his wife and marriage.

As the sixth call ended without being picked up, Bina and Abhimanyu had asked for self-restraint and longevity; and facilitative seasons worldwide.

For the seventh time, Feroze called, and by then, Bina and Abhimanyu had sworn to be friends for life, living together as faithful companions with compassion, loyalty and unity, not only for themselves but for the peace of the cosmos as well.

* * *

Feroze was delirious. He threw his phone away, it hit a wall with a loud whack, but the sound paled miserably in audibility compared to the silence of loss that arose from within him. He had no idea the marriage was taking place in Sadhu Belo, or else he would have barged into the area. It was only a short distance from where he lived.

He cried like an abandoned baby, ineffective and unconsoled.

Later, in the dead of night, feeling like a rabid bat, Feroze picked up his phone again and called Bina. It was only for the sake of it; he knew all had ended already.

Hashmatullah's law had failed again on him. Between fuck-or-get-fucked, he had again ended up on the wrong side.

A phone on silent mode lit in a dark room a few miles south of where the call was coming from; two people lay sleeping on the bed beside it. Some hours ago, a holy union had taken place right there. Two people had become, physically and spiritually, one.

The fire had witnessed it.

The cosmos had designed it.

But the cosmos...

Chapter Twenty Three

WHEN BINA woke up, the sun had already blanketed the city with its light that twinkled with heat. Wearily, she spread her hand out to find her phone, which she found lying on the edge of the bed. She tapped her finger on the screen, which lit up to announce 21 missed calls. Must have been from her colleagues and peers, congratulating her on her marriage. Most had already told her they wouldn't be able to make it to the ceremony, Sukkur was way too far away, and people from Islamabad, anyway, pretended that even the short journey to adjoining Rawalpindi was nothing less than an ordeal for them. She did not check the calls.

Bina slowly got out of bed and readjusted the duvet as she stood up. Abhimanyu was in a state of deep slumber on the other side of the bed, naked, his head immersed in a pillow with his arms stretched out.

She went to the bathroom to wash herself, brushed her teeth, and changed into a saari: a banarasi red piece that had the edges smouldered in black. She wasn't accustomed to wearing saaris; she had only tried them as an experience during *Navratri* once, back when she lived in Sukkur. She went to the dresser, and sat before it. The makeup still hadn't fallen off completely; it smudged the sides of her eyes and lips; she simply covered it with a new layer. And after thinking for a while, she put a *tilak* on her forehead.

Homecoming.

Her banishment - the *banbaas* - had ended.

She had stopped wearing these after she left Sukkur; there was no need to flaunt who she was like that, Shreeshanth had told her. They blended with the area in Sukkur almost naturally, but the Punjabi heartlands weren't used to seeing these symbols of identity - at least for 75 years.

Bina hadn't given it much thought then, but Shreeshanth was so resistant to the idea that Bina wasn't accustomed to seeing her father so adamant. She acquiesced; the issue was so petty for her that it didn't warrant picking a fight with her father over. Shreeshanth, after all, had never told Bina he had named her so, only so she could pass the question of identity without raising many eyebrows.

Bina.

A safe word.

Doesn't give away too much.

* * *

A gaggle of all the family guests occupied the house's verandah, having their brunch, and talking to each other in booming notes. There were about fifteen people in total, minus the kids, who were the actual source of nuisance in the setting. Shreeshanth was calling out for everyone to be served to their full capacity. Kamla *Bua* ran around with Aarti to cater to the essentials; the help they had hired for the wedding being dictated about by them. Rashmi, Kamla's younger daughter, had turned into a girl. Bina stopped to recognise the uncanny resemblance she bore with Sharda, and a wound gaped. When Bina reached Sukkur a few days ago for her marriage, she had asked Kamla *Bua* where Sharda was in such a big event in her sister's life. The unconfined emotion settled in a jiffy; they both knew the answer.

Mehar and Aariz sat at the far end of the table. Bina had asked Aariz to stay for another day.

177

"Tomorrow, we have a sightseeing plan as well." Aariz, who had done enough sightseeing in his life, didn't buy the idea at first. But when Mehar asked him to stay and that they could return to Lahore together a day later, he had agreed.

The people at the table were excitable; they had plans for the day. Sure enough, they had come to bless the couple's union, but people in this part of the world don't attend weddings for that reason solely. Everyone has too much to do and too little time. Getting more punch out of one thing is always a good idea. They were supposed to see the city after the brunch, where the newly married Bina was to be their guide. Abhimanyu's family had never been to Sukkur before. In fact, they had never been above the imaginary boundary where their desert in the South ended. Mehar had also never seen Sukkur before. Those who had seen the city were still eager to go out; it might relax their hyperactive kids.

Half an hour later, the coaster they had hired arrived, and they all left. Bina entered last. Walking around in a saari tested every nerve of her body.

* * *

Even when Mehar had told Bina to lay low and act like a bride - coy and shy - only to partake in something which Bina had never experienced in her life before, the fights-and-rights Bina couldn't help it. The roar of the coaster's engine and Bina's vocal cords assumed life in precisely the same go.

"Welcome to my city, everyone," she started.

"Is the plane about to take off?" Aariz joked.

"Anyway," Bina ignored him. "Sukkur is the third largest city of Sindh. And as you can see, it's a darling."

"If beauty lies in the eyes of the beholder, mine don't have any." Aariz pointed out to the strip of dry land they were passing by.

"Duly ignored," Bina retorted. "It's difficult to say how old this city is, but the ruins of Lakhanjo-daro attest that it has been inhabited for some millennia. People know about Mohenjodaro, but this settlement goes back to the same Indus Valley Civilization. However, the modern recordings of the city start essentially with the British period, which elevated its position, surpassing the erstwhile important centres of Shikarpur and Larkana."

"Larkano," Feroze would always call it. He had always been more loyal to the king than the king himself.

The fear of not fully belonging.

"Thank you, Wikipedia," Aariz said. Bina made a face at him.

They continued in the banter for quite some time, before the coaster screeched and went dead.

They had reached their first destination.

"We are at Sukkur barrage," Bina told them even when they all had guessed it already. "Don't go too far!" she yelled at a relative's child. "It controls one of the largest irrigation systems in the world. This, and the railway network, are probably some of the greatest things to remember the British by in Sukkur." Abhimanyu looked at the barrage dreamily. He always romanticised the excess of water, given that he came from a parched land. Aariz wasn't paying much attention.

"Tell me about the people here, Bina." Mehar was interested.

"Different ethnicities have settled here over the years; sometimes, it is hard to tell where one ends and the other begins. Before the creation of Pakistan, though, Sukkur was a Hindu city, seventy per cent of its population was Hindu, but the number had decreased to two per cent in four years after that."

"Was it due to the riots?" Aariz asked casually.

Mehar remembered one Satnam Singh who had always lived with her but she had never met.

"Not really; unlike Punjab, very few Hindus were killed in Sindh during partition. Sindhi Muslims had unanimously refused the calls to turn against their Hindu neighbours." Bina paused, and Feroze suddenly came to her mind. "But riots broke out in 1948 in Karachi; they were local and directed against the Punjabi Sikhs seeking refuge in Karachi. That inculcated fear in Hindus as well, and they left en masse."

Had Satnam Singh gone to Karachi? Was he killed there? Or had he left for the other Punjab and lived? Mehar's mind had trailed off.

Some minutes later, they all passed through the Lab-e-Mehran, the sprawling blotch of green beside the Indus. Mehar liked the place; it was serene. The kids had run off to play dodge-the-ball towards the side, their parents hitting them with the balls they had brought, with enough force to shake the kids but not enough to hurt them.

Bina looked at the Indus and whispered to Mehar; Aariz and Abhimanyu were a little off in the distance, talking, "It's so strange that the same thing has different definitions if you change the context, Mehar. The Indus passes through Punjab as well. But in Punjab, it is just a river for me. In Sindh, it's a god."

After they had had refreshments and the kids were tired and sweaty, they left. They crossed the bazar of Neem Ki Chari and passed Masoom Shah Jo Minaro, the tower of Masoom Shah. "It was a watchtower built during the Mughal period," Bina told them from inside the coaster. "But Masoom Shah passed away during the construction and was buried under an incomplete tower."

"Who was Masoom Shah?" Abhimanyu asked.

"A governor during the reign of Mughal Emperor Akbar."

Mehar was reminded of another governor of the Mughal era: Wazir Khan.

"Have you heard from Feroze?" Aariz asked Bina, careful no one was listening to them. Bina shook her head furtively.

A while later, they reached Satyaan Jo Astaan, the abode of seven. Bina had, over the years, become wary of shrines, of how Sindh was almost fetishised by the concept of Sufis and their shrines, because what was said and practised had obscene discrepancies. All of this represented to her a guileful scheme to abdicate people. The shrines came with their own baggage:

political and religious dynasties that had no correlation with the verses of the saints that slept inside. But she never gave up on visiting; she retained her cultural identity while downplaying her religious one. Bina quickly told the men the story of this shrine before proceeding towards it with Mehar, as only women were allowed inside. "There were seven pious women once who were being chased by a prince who wanted to abduct them. They reached this spot and, having nowhere to go, prayed to the Earth to take them in. And it swallowed them."

Aariz had heard stories like this before as well.

When they were done with seeing most of what the city offered, all of them retired to the bank of Indus, where they could see the famous bridge in the distance. Two kids used to come here many years ago, to make stories about cars and waxed lyrical about this mighty river and the magic it carried. The four people sat on the ground, boats bellowing to board them in the distance.

"It was constructed by the viceroy of India. It is an engineering marvel." Bina sounded tired, finally. "And there's a newer bridge with it as well. Ayub bridge."

Below the bridge, they could see the shrine of Zinda Pir. The coaster driver silently came towards the bank and prayed towards it. Abhimanyu and Bina were used to this practice, as were Aariz and Mehar, but slightly.

"Zinda Pir is a mystery. A man who was and is, who is demanding to be described in any simple way. And there are various miracles related to him. It is said that during the 1965 war, India wanted to bomb this bridge. But the Zinda Pir came up, started catching the bombs and throwing them into the water."

Mehar had heard stories like this before as well.

The ends of the sky had forged a pink lustre; Bina reclined on Abhimanyu's shoulder and closed her eyes. Assured that they were protected by the dark, Abhimanyu slipped his hand inside the drape of Bina's saari and fondled her breast. She jerked it brusquely; it landed near her waist where the skin was the smoothest, and started caressing the path that led downward before Bina held it, smiling.

It had been a good day. Bina had not been to these places in a very long time, even when they constituted a large part of who she was. It was like meeting different versions of herself contained in time, accepting them, and becoming a whole. She did not know how long it would be before she saw these places again.

Aariz looked at Mehar, and they smiled at each other.

The Indus spread into a vast expanse before them, before it became nothing and transpired into the air. It had been on the run for millennia, never stopping, only observing the people who had been coming to visit it for all these years, their faces changing after every few decades. It smiled with vain glory over the significance it held over its people. It was the primary source of their livelihood, the people worshipped it, made stories about it, but every once in a while, when the Indus would tire of its monotony, it would take the shape of vagrant floods and decimate everything.

Indus the creator, Indus the destroyer.

Ending something, and beginning another.

* * *

On the way back, Bina suddenly remembered another fascinating bit she had forgotten to tell her friends. She told them that they were not sure about its stability after the British finished constructing the bridge connecting Sukkur to Rohri. So they filled a train with convicts marked for capital punishment; their crimes were varied, but all were of the gravity qualifying them to be killed. These people were set off on the train over the bridge. They were as liable to fall into the river to their deaths as they were to survive. As the train passed over the bridge, it rattled. The convicts were afraid, but the bridge stood. As a celebration of this marvel, the government freed all the convicts.

But it clearly wasn't Bina's place to tell them that some years between these two incidents, another train had left from Amritsar to reach Wagah. These people were also convicts but of a different kind. Their crime was being the wrong people in the wrong place at the wrong time. As they seated themselves in the train to Pakistan, they were relieved; it would only be some time before they would be freed from the dread of being killed. But by the time the train crossed Wagah, all the people inside it were already dead. Butchered in cold blood, their heads were lying with the feet of others, and babies were lying in the blood of their mothers' hearts.

Two trains started their journeys in different places, and different times, and with different people, but the pilgrimages ended very differently for both of them.

So between these, whose pilgrimage was successful?

Who can say?

* * *

There is more than one way to tell a story. Because human recollection, like human understanding and reasoning, is a biased, fallible idea. We often think we know a story only because we know how it climaxes. And there's another way to tell the story that four people shared with each other that day.

In a dry land with no name and where the concept of time and space has ceased to exist, a woman strides restlessly and forth; she knows she has to do something, but where does she start?

The woman's name is Bina.

After walking for a few days just like that, she one day spots a robust and muscular man coming toward her from the corner of her eye. She is timid at first, but he gives off a good vibe. He approaches her and extends his hand toward her.

"My name is Feroze. We have recently come here and have taken over to develop this land. I will also become the prince of this land in a few years. I have heard you are also interested in making a proper city here?"

For a while, Bina is apprehensive. This is her land, and Feroze speaks a language different from hers. How can he be the prince? But she needs help anyway.

"We need to make this place accessible so people can come here. It's cut off from elsewhere currently."

"I know what to do."

As they walk towards the distance, another man joins them. Feroze introduces him to Bina.

"He is Aariz. He is a friend." But Bina finds Feroze's pronunciation of "friend" a little unsettling.

After reaching a point in the middle of nowhere, Feroze picks up a stick and puts it on the ground.

"A railway will run through here." He starts marking a line on the ground.

Bina does not like the idea. "But a line will divide the city."

"We have no other way; it has been decided by my elders who are in charge now," Feroze says; his friend Aariz doesn't say a word.

And they start building a railway there.

And the city gets its railway network.

People start coming to the city, loads of them. They come from far-off places and are ranged in their complexion and build. One day, a train stops before them, and a woman emerges.

"I have been forced out of my home, and they locked the gates. Can I stay here?" she entreats the three people, but there's steadfastness in her voice.

"What is your name?"

"Mehar."

"Where have you come from, Mehar?"

"From a place far from here. It has many monuments and gardens. Do you have any of those here?"

The three people look down at the ground.

"Let's build them, then. There, besides the river. We'll make a garden and add a monument to it later," Mehar says.

She goes to the place and starts building a garden. As the other people approach her to extend help, she stops them. "I am used to doing things on my own. And this is an easy task; I have been through a lot worse."

And the city gets its Lab-e-Mehran.

As the four people are frolicking in the park one day, another person comes to them. He is dark and thinly built.

The person introduces himself as Abhimanyu.

"I have been sent by the masters here. They want to construct a bridge over the river so that it helps the people and makes lives easier for them. I will construct it."

Bina loves the idea. She is palpably eager. Feroze looks at her, overjoyed, and scoffs at Abhimanyu.

"You will not be able to build it."

"I will be."

And he does it.

He names it after his masters.

And the city gets its Lansdowne Bridge.

Aariz, Bina, and Mehar applaud Abhimanyu's effort. They all have warmed up to him, on which Feroze gets angry.

"I will do something that this man cannot do. I will show you something you've not seen before. I will build a 500 feet long barrage, irrigating more than ten million acres of land," he tells the people angrily.

And the city gets its barrage.

Aariz looks at it and comments, "I don't think it's a good idea to control rivers like that. You're setting yourself up for calamities: floods and droughts."

Mehar finds Aariz's idea gripping but doesn't speak. She is fixated on building her monument.

"The bridge is still crucial." Abhimanyu looks at Feroze; Bina has a slight hint of agreement in her sight.

Feroze gets furious. "I will make a bridge also, which is better than yours." He does and names it after his great grandfather.

And the city gets its Ayub bridge.

Feroze is jubilant. But he is still unable to get the unanimous applause of the crowd. His friend Aariz is not giving him much attention. And the women still seem to be impressed with Abhimanyu. Suddenly, they hear a group of seven women coming out of the water. Feroze knows this is his time to cement his dominance.

He runs after them, and the four other people chase him. Bina catches sight of one of the people in the running group of women. It's a child. She thinks she knows her; she might have been her sister.

"Feroze, stop!" the three of them shout, but Aariz responds, "He will not. No one taught him how to. And it's already too late for any teaching."

The women finally reach a spot where they cannot escape from. They look back at Feroze approaching them and pray for the Earth to take them in.

It does.

Bina screams, and Mehar consoles her.

"Why doesn't the Earth swallow you as well and punish you?" Abhimanyu shouts at Feroze.

"His life will be his punishment, but he doesn't know it yet," Aariz says, feeling sympathetic towards his friend.

And the city gets its Satyaan Jo Astaan.

The women are furious at Feroze, and they stop talking to him. Aariz and Abhimanyu are detached from the group.

"I want a monument," Mehar says after a few days.

"I will build a monument for you," Aariz tells her.

He starts building a tower. None of what has happened here has made any sense to him. So he wants to construct something elevated; maybe it will give him a bird's eye view of things, and he will be able to see that things around the place have some method to their madness.

All of them have cut off Feroze. The four people gather at a point, and Aariz starts constructing a tower. Mehar is happy, but midway, Aariz gets tired.

"I want to sleep. I am knackered. I'll just rest here under this tower."

Aariz sleeps, and he doesn't wake up for many years. The three people give him a blanket of mud to keep him warm.

"What do we call this tower?"

"Aariz had such innocence in his eyes," Mehar responds.

And the city gets its Masoom Shah Jo Minaro.

The four people sit by the bank of the river. Their city is complete, and they are all tired for the excessive efforts all of them have put into realising it.

"But what do we call this city?" Bina asks.

Feroze approaches out of nowhere and suggests a name.

"No way," Bina reacts. "That is an Arabic name; I am not Arabic. I am an Indoi, an Indus person."

"It does not matter. Every language is the same, or will become so," replies Feroze.

Bina is not convinced and looks at Abhimanyu to get his opinion. He only shrugs. After a while, Mehar holds her hand and says, "But the word also means sukh."

Happiness.

Bina likes it now. They all agree on the name.

And the city gets its name: Sukkur.

Chapter Twenty Four

ONE MONTH later, inside the second floor of an aged, squinted house in the Old City of Lahore, sat a Laal Pari in front of a mirror, three of the neighbourhood women with her, while her friend Bina - recently married and "glowing" as everyone teased her - was occupied with arranging for the affair. Of course, she wouldn't let anyone else take the lead on such an important day; she was the fights-and-rights Bina. Nashmia applied red lipstick to the Pari's lips, careful not to deform the borders, and put an artificial necklace around a slender neck; she might have picked a quarrel with Bina over assuming the post of in charge, but her assignments were already keeping her gainfully busy. The women looked at each other and sneered, before they caught sight of the Laal Pari looking at them and went back to putting kohl in her eyes. A large red dupatta, shining at the edges with golden lace that frilled at the edges, was put on her head; it hung in front of her face and covered her eyes. She made for a striking figure; no one had really noticed her beauty before - somehow, beauty also seems more fitting when it comes from money. Bina came forward to look at the bride and kissed her.

"You are the most beautiful bride I have ever seen."

Laal Pari was going to be married that day.

In the lanes that surrounded her house, people were hushed up about the subject. It was a complex event they were having trouble decoding all the layers of. There was an undertone of reverence about the day, as if an *urs* was about to commence, as Chacha Abdul Kareem had told them.

Some people were a little aggrieved; they had grown so convinced about the blessings the Laal Pari carried about herself that they thought a charm of protection was being snatched away from them. Others wanted to glance at her but did not know the terms of reference for such a liberty.

The marriage was a pretty simple affair. The groom had brought a *maulvi* with them, who read through some verses in Arabic and asked them if they accepted the other as their spouse.

Yes.

And again.

And then again.

The woman's family members sat by their sides, only her brother and sister-in-law (*Abba* had refused to come, Amma had refused to disobey *Abba's* orders, and Asad *Bhai* was under the weather) offering everyone sweets as the *nikah* was done. The man only had some friends with him. They cracked a few jokes, and that was it. He had invited Feroze as well, who had been unreachable. Even if he had read the texts, he had not responded.

The man and the woman were legally, officially, and religiously married right then. Everyone congratulated them. Some women sobbed: it was a ritual they had practised for as long as the Mughal monuments had stood around them. Or maybe, even before that.

And there was another ritual that came to play. While they were signing their marriage papers, the question of the dower arose—something that a husband has to give his wife in Islamic tradition. What will this financially well-off man from Modern Lahore give to their prized daughter of Old Lahore? Everyone swooped down upon the couple to get the details: the women, the men, even the children. It wasn't just a transaction between two people; for them, it was a social experiment determining how their Lahore fared against the other.

"It should be two million at least, and does the boy own any land?" One woman whispered to another.

"Talha works only as a delivery boy, but even he wrote 5 lacs for my daughter, Chammo," said another.

The tension was rising; it was as if the money written on the papers was a lot more crucial for everyone else than the couple itself. Mehar looked at Aariz, and he said something to the maulvi that, to the discomfiture of the audience, was audible only to the maulvi. The slight twitch in the maulvi's profile suggested that even he was looking for more, but he got down to writing on the papers. When he was done scribbling, Mehar's brother saw what was written:

Umrah.

While Mehar could have asked Aariz for anything, she only wanted him to be her fellow pilgrim.

Her dower was only a religious pilgrimage.

The heart wants what it wants.

There was no space for parking around the woman's house, not even to bring a car nearby, so the couple had to walk the way to where the car was parked, near the Royal Bath. As they both made their way towards it, people around them took the opportunity to gleefully look at their Laal Pari. Some people threw flowers at the couple walking below them from the upper storey windows of their houses. One man came out of the blue and touched the woman's feet. The woman took a step back, stunned. Her groom observed blankly. As they neared the car, a misty-eyed Chacha Abdul Kareem appeared and blessed the woman, putting his hand on her head.

"Stay blessed, my child!"

She smiled; tears developed out of nothingness and started swimming in her eyes. She thanked him without saying a word.

They had to wait in the car for a while because the Delhi Gate was getting some of its frescoes redone that day. Offices were being established inside the gate of a government body to be in charge of the area. But after a while, they cleared the spot, removing the wooden planks and iron foliage from the mouth of the gate, and opened it.

They left.

* * *

As Aariz lived alone, there was no one to welcome them to their home, except for Zainab. On the night of their marriage, Aariz and Mehar sat silently across from each other. The intimacy they shared couldn't be comprehended by many. It went beyond the carnal desires, and knocked at the realm of the unknown.

Their bond was special, almost ancient.

It was a bond that men have had with their angels, that the believers have had with their souls, that the Sufis have had with their hearts.

It was so much and so little.

An escape as well as homecoming.

It was a bond so complete that it would always remain incomplete. Both enjoying each other's shadows but never sharing their stems.

Oil and Water.

Aariz and Mehar did not have to tell each other that there would never be a physical relationship between them; one's decision came from a lack of want, the other's, from having catered too much to want.

They knew.

They understood.

* * *

Zainab used to come to clean and cook daily to their apartment, every morning at eight, leaving by two to pick up her son from school. She was strangely amused by the couple in the months she worked for them. She had never really seen anyone like them. They were different, the only ones of their sort. She had never seen them fight, or quibble; they would just easily merge into the other seamlessly. They were not your typical husband and wife in any way, and that unsettled Zainab. It opened the possibilities of what-could-have-been for Zainab, before she brought herself back to certitude and told herself that such adventures often lead to mortification. Society has devised its ways over a thousand years, and it is silly to mess with them. Those who had done so were either hung, drowned, or walled alive.

To Zainab, the couple was dysfunctional.

To itself, the couple was utterly functional.

* * *

Mehar turned on the music on her phone, and Muhammad Rafi's voice broke out.

"Khoya Khoya Chand,

Khula Aasmaan,

Tum ko bhi kaisay neend ayegi?

Ankhon mein saari raat jayegi..."

The lost moon and the open sky,

The whole night will fly before your eyes,

How will you be able to sleep?

This song brought back so many memories. It transported her into the past, to a particular juncture where history met the present, and both became the same. Of a time when she would fly kites and beat boys. Of a time when she would become one with the Mughal motifs and arches. Of a time when she would excel through her school tests, and fire paper bullets off a rubber band entangled around her fingers on the other students. Of a time when this song would present the prospects of a vast, untried world to a little girl.

Of a time when fathers had not yet become men and husbands had not yet become pimps.

She let herself sway to the song slightly. Aariz, sitting on the bed, didn't register. He was so used to the sound of this song that it now formed routine background music in his life, even when he did not listen to Bollywood songs otherwise. Mehar looked at him and smiled. Aariz remained consumed with working on his laptop. Mehar went towards the window, lit a cigarette, and looked at the moon. It was on to becoming a whole, round ball; it shone bright that night.

Mehar = sun.

So much is lost in translation, she thought. A specific language changes the character of the same thing. She wondered if the light of the moon would exactly be the same in the lanes of the Old City as it was here. The moon could be the same, or not, but she knew the Mehar was different. The music was different as well. Mohammad Rafi sounded different in the two places.

Outside in the city, things went on as per the routine. Cars in a chase after each other, each willing to scurry past the other in a bid to reach their destinations first and do nothing, leaving behind a trail of multi-coloured lights on the ever-increasing underpasses and fly-overs of the city, people grouping in the dark of the night to execute a plan of robbery or occupying the land of one of their relatives who had gone abroad, teenage people texting their crushes inappropriate messages and smiling on getting inviting replies, friends chatting away their lives happily in the chic cafes of the cities ready to snatch the bill as it came, people waking up for *tahajudd* prayers and crying to God for the things they really needed, people sleeping after the failures of another day - recharging themselves for the drudgery of yet another day, babies waking their parents in the middle of the night, the perplexed parents taking it on each other, not knowing what the problem is now, hospitals working round the clock at full capacity, oblivious to the concept of night. Someone has rushed in with his heavily pregnant wife, bellowing at the doctors to attend to her, someone has had a daughter, and is now hoping he can rewind destiny, someone is distributing confections on the birth of a baby, while someone trembles with despair over the death of his neonate who had been in the incubator for two days.

Babies being born.

Babies going dead.

The beginning of one thing.

The end of another.

* * *

When Aariz came out of the shower, a towel around his waist, and his body coated in an envelope of evaporating steam, the vision of Mehar stopped him in his tracks. The air in the room was viscous.

She was sitting on the fringe of the bed, her naked back facing him. Her head had fallen to her chest, which she held in her hands, and her hair spread out. Time stood frozen around her.

When she felt his presence in the room, she turned back to look at him. She called him towards her, and he went.

She stood up gradually, taking Aariz's hands into her own, and motioned for him to sit beside her.

Her eyes appeared to be empty; tears had washed away everything they had carried before. Two vessels whose cargo had been burgled.

Mehar slowly put her head on Aariz's naked chest, where she could feel his heart beating. His skin smelled of water, and comfort.

She gradually tightened her grip on his hand and brought it to her body. His hand brushed against her belly, her navel; her skin reacting in slight spasms where he touched her; before she finally placed his palm on her lower abdomen.

He knew.

He understood.

Once, there had been a life there. A tiny heart had beaten inside. Some little limbs had started forming there. She was unsure if a soul had taken residence in the little body growing inside her, but she had felt its presence. It had consumed her.

After a while, Mehar said, barely audible to Aariz, "It was a girl. I would have named her Sakina."

Aariz listened, intently, lending her the support of his touch.

She had done the most sacred thing a person can do on the planet: create life.

And then she had killed it.

She had done the most profane thing a person can do on the planet: end life.

But it is for the clergy and philosophers to decide what is sacred, creating or protecting life? Especially if you have to end a life to protect it?

What is defensible and what is not?

Aariz felt the warmth being emanated from her body. She breathed in heaves, the tears from her eyes falling on his body and sliding past it. A river started flowing, it became a flood and drowned everything, but an Ark led them to safety. He put his other hand on her waist. They sat like that, touching each other, their wet skins a conduit.

Her grief passed over from her body and brushed against his, settling between them. All the words in the universe seemed redundant; their mode of communication had failed all other ways. They knew they would not need anything else from each other after this. A curtain fell. The end: sanctuary and safety; the words appeared before the curtain. The choreography the cosmos had designed for them had reached its climax. The angels stood up to clap, and the invisible audience gave them a standing ovation. It was a ritual that set them free.

Azadi.

Freedom.

The marriage was consummated.

Chapter Twenty Five

FOR BINA and Abhimanyu, their marriage turned out to be a perfect setting of convenience. It had been months since their marriage, but they did not have to make any momentous adjustments; the pieces fit themselves automatically. Abhimanyu's demureness was snugly offset by Bina's boldness. Abhimanyu had moved to Islamabad with Bina, where he took a job in the office of the NGO for which he worked. It was a city he was astounded by but knew he could never be inured to. They were, anyway, working on plans for their future; and relegated to life the autonomy of taking them to new places.

Bina packed certain essential items in her hand carry. She would start packing days before any future trip, and she waited for Abhimanyu to come out of the room and stuff some of his things inside her bag. And then there were trips before the trip, the urgent detours she had to make through the country before going on a foreign tour with Abhimanyu.

The first journey was going to be a long drive, all the way from Islamabad to Sukkur, but the road was acceptable. And this, anyway, wasn't a route she wasn't conditioned to. She had spent her life commuting, vacillating between places, getting tattered a little at every terminus.

When Feroze invited Bina for dinner at his place, emerging out of thin air to loom over her life after being away for months, she was initially reluctant. He had also not shown up at her wedding, or Mehar and Aariz's. He had told her he had been unwell and was admitted to a hospital.

Regarding the invitation, it was only a few days before she and Abhimanyu flew out of the country, and there was too much to do. Down with the people who portray travelling as sexy - it's a bother. There is so much to do that something always remains to be done: a checklist of neverending ticks. She wondered if Abhimanyu had converted the rupees into euros, and she anticipated a negative answer. She had tried to explain it to Feroze, but knew he would not understand the conundrum.

Bina did not want to make that journey. It was one station the train had diverted its track from.

But then it was Feroze.

And if closure really was what Bina sought, there could not be a better opportunity.

How many closures will we seek, Aariz had asked.

Feroze had begged, and was averse to the idea of him coming to see her. Like a spoiled kid, he still dictated the rules of the game. And started crying foul otherwise. Or breaking the toys. In cricket as well, when they were kids, every ball hitting the wickets would be tagged as a "test ball" by Feroze.

Typical Feroze.

"For old times' sake," he had said.

She would do a lot for old times' sake.

For Feroze's sake.

Having dinner in his house was the least of them.

* * *

In sixteenth-century India, a woman hailed from the Royal Rajput family of Kudki. Once, she saw the statue of Krishna, and that was it for her. The woman called Meerabai lost her heart to Krishna, and spent all her life trying to be one with him. She took him to be her husband, and even when she married the crown prince of Mewar, her heart remained emblazoned with the dark one. It is said that after her husband died, she left for the wilderness: to write poetry for Krishna.

"I danced before my *Giridhara*. Again and again, I dance..." She denounced all she had and became an ardent devotee of the god she thought she was married to. Persecution followed, most often by her in-laws, but Krishna would always watch over her. The mystic wandered in her journey of union with *Murlimahonar*, never deterred by the antagonism that came her way but followed the flute of Krishna that hummed in her blood.

The heart wants what it wants.

But Krishna wasn't Meera's. He was Radha's, millennia before Meera was born. And history testifies to this; they are named and worshipped together. Growing up in Vrindavan among the *gopis*, Radha and Krishna's love was known far and beyond. Radha would come flying to the sound of her lover's music and dance; Krishna's mischiefs being the constant in her life. Then Krishna left; the cosmos had designed other things for him. But it is claimed that a special type of marriage, the *Gandharva*, was performed between Radha and Krishna. The marriage of hearts. Either way, their story had already been immortalised for what it was.

Between Radha and Meera, whose love was stronger?

Is attainable love more real or forbidden love?

Is love about holding on or letting go?

Who can say?

Meera lived her last days in either Dwarka or Vrindavan, the abodes of Krishna, and she died by becoming one with a statue of Krishna.

Want is a strange thing.

But those are stories from another era. Radha is worshipped. Meera is honoured. All for the simple act of love and devotion? Who will worship the current devotees and lovers? Who will celebrate or remember them? Those who still wander in the desert, knowing they can never get their Krishna but are unyielding. Who will write stories about them?

Or will they die, nameless, faceless?

Time is a continuum.

The faces change. The names change.

The eternal idea of the universe continues to the same tune.

Tick, tick, tick...

* * *

When Bina was gearing up for her trip, Aariz and Mehar were already mid-way through theirs. They had gone to Saudi Arabia for the Umrah pilgrimage, as the payment of Mehar's dower to her. It wasn't exactly planned, but it was convenient to add it as it was something they had already professed to do. Aariz had to go to Dubai to score a deal with potential investors from the Middle East, and they decided to fly to Medina before returning home.

After their marriage, their travelling plans had seen a setback as the country had been ravaged by dreadful floods. Aariz took Mehar to the north, though, they went to Chitral, where they stayed with Qaiser Kalasha in his wooden house in the Bamburet Valley that was three hundred years old. Mehar, who had rarely been out of Lahore, found this most intimate; she learned much more about Aariz by living the places he had been to. Qaiser shared the secrets of their community that they were skittish about sharing publicly.

On the current trip, they had stayed in Medina for three days and were now on their way to Makkah.

Their bus driver pushed the brakes a little outside of Makkah. They were to change into *ehraams,* the sacred state they were supposed to enter before proceeding further. Mehar and Aariz got out of the bus. It was sunset, and the last rays of the drowning sun were being played around by the hoary, dry mountains and the desert land that ignited like a gold mine. It was a scene to be collared in memory.

About fourteen hundred years ago, another man had made this journey too. He had been forced out of his motherland and was set to return to Mecca after living in Medina for eight years. The man had been ostracised, ridiculed, and tortured by the people of Mecca. Some members of his family had also been slain remorselessly. The thorns had been plentiful on his path to love with the supreme. Every step of the ladder of proclaiming that love was met with torment. He was repeatedly told he would be spared the agony only if he kept his love to himself; the public spectacle was the issue most had with it.

Is hidden love as worthy as open love?

Is love dictated by rules, or does it dictate them?

Who can say?

But one thing was confusing: after turning the winds around in his favour, he sought no blood even after being bloodied. He sought no vengeance even after being hurt. He did not want to do what had been done to him.

Want is a strange thing.

And so he returned, to Mecca. To a city that was once his home, his hearth - that now lay fallen before him. Would he let his 10,000 men strong army loose to do as they pleased with the people who had once been so unkind to him? The Meccans feared. But he decided the cycle of spite had to be smashed somewhere. He instead chose to speak the kind words that Prophet Yusuf had once said to his brothers. He told all those gathered before him, afraid, that Mecca was a sanctuary. He told them that he forgave them for what they had done and that they were now free to go their ways.

Conquerors decimate cities.

He embraced it.

Did Mecca fall?

Did Mecca rise?

About fourteen hundred years later, as numerous people make

the same journey between these two holy cities that defines so much, they are still at a loss.

They are still looking for their kind words, sanctuaries, forgivers, and freedom.

Time is a continuum.

The people change. The cities change.

The eternal quest of the universe continues to the same tune.

Tick, tick, tick...

Chapter Twenty Six

AFTER THEIR return from Umrah, Aariz and Mehar stayed for a night in Islamabad, where their flight was scheduled. Bina and Abhimanyu had rented a place in one of the capital's new, peripheral sectors and had invited Aariz and Mehar to stay with them. They had agreed. Bina and Abhimanyu drove to pick them up from the airport, and got them out of the arrivals lounge, which was brimming with joyous family members and teary relatives. It was Mehar's first time in Islamabad; for a moment, she couldn't believe that her tangy, cluttered neighbourhood and this broad, glistening city existed in the same country. This stark contrast was almost disparaging.

And where were the monuments?

After resting for a couple of hours, the four people sat together for dinner. Bina had cooked, and Aariz laughed that marriage had made a typical woman out of her. Bina laughed, "over my dead body."

Mehar gleefully observed that Bina and Abhimanyu were a fit together. They both had the same interests, same temperament, and same outlook on life, even if Bina's was more radical. This equation worked all the better; Abhimanyu's submissive attitude made Bina's dominance the fitting ingredient in the recipe, not causing any friction between them. In the dining room, a portrait of *Jhulelaal* looked over the dishes being served. Aariz ate a little,

Mehar a lot. Abhimanyu had already eaten, and Bina always counted her calories.

Soon enough, Bina and Aariz entered into a conversation, as they usually did. The interest of the two other participants in the meeting ranged from one to five.

"How's everyone back home, Bina?"

"Everyone's good. The parents have returned to Sukkur after our failed efforts to move them to Karachi, where Rinkle lives. They said they couldn't adjust to the city's feverish pace and couldn't be too far from the Indus and their lives. Rinkle had a son last month."

"Congratulations. We have been so consumed with so much these months that we haven't gotten a chance to discuss the details."

"That is true. But it's not like we've ever done that before either. We'd be so busy talking about your scholarly adventures that we usually kept to that."

"Or your heroism," Aariz smiled. Mehar and Abhimanyu joined in agreement. One knew Bina before, and the other had gotten to know her well.

Bina gave a dry laugh and continued in the same good humour, "We don't need heroes in this country, Aariz. Heroes are fallible. We just need some god-forsaken sane people."

"Good luck finding any."

"Not everyone can give up on the world, Aariz. There's so much to cherish here as well. And we are responsible for changing things even if they seem minor."

"We?" Aariz raised an eyebrow. Abhimanyu smiled.

"We have discussed this so many times before; we just look at things differently." Bina was serious.

"You think certain things need saving. I think everything is beyond saving."

"There we go with your existential angst again. Now it has become a recurring soap opera," Bina shrugged her shoulders.

"But it sure garners some ratings."

Mehar started pouring tea into the cups.

"You know I admire your courage, Bina. You've always been the one to take a stand. But I just fear that there might come a time when you'll realise nothing was worth it. And you cannot put this down to only my nihilism." Aariz was stringent for the first time in the conversation.

"That is a pretty subjective thing, Aariz," Abhimanyu spoke for the first time.

"Yes, that is," Bina agreed. "And everything is worth it, Aariz. Do you know of all the cases I became a witness to in the forced abduction cases? Two girls returned. Most didn't, but at least it signalled that people had the victims' backs. Our conservation drives regarding the temples of Nagarparkar met with a certain level of success. Now that I am a party to what Abhimanyu does, you should see how you change a life by giving someone access to water in an arid desert. Let's leave that; just doing my routine job is also making a change; the simple act of fixing a dislocated shoulder which is a simple routine for me, is changing someone else's life. You cannot say that nothing is worth it."

"The injustices will continue, the waters will again dry up, and shoulders will keep on being broken," Aariz retorted.

"So the solution you have is to look the other way? We need to contribute, in whatever capacity, and your opinions come from a place of disconnected privilege."

"We all come from our own places. You do the work because it makes you feel important. That is your drive."

"No, Aariz. You should be the last person to tell me I do this because of who I am. I'm not some stereotypical Hindu girl whose claim to fame is selling her marginalisation and asking for aid, even though many may want to portray me like that."

"I know that, Bina. I never said you were. All I am saying is every selfless act is essentially a selfish act. We do it because it is good for us. Otherwise, what happens around is too big and chaotic to be affected by what we do."

"That again is one way to look at it, Aariz. It might give

me a sense of purpose; that part is true. But what should be the alternative? Forfeiture? Acceptance? Putting everything on a great plan? The design of the cosmos?"

Abhimanyu often nodded at what Bina said; Mehar couldn't bring herself to side with either party; she was used to such a heated exchange of ideas between the friends.

"Just living the reality is also a feat in itself. Understanding - without judgement - is key. Exerting our effect only disrupts the routine of what is bound to happen."

"No, I might as well leave an imprint if I am here. And that doesn't essentially have to be something mammoth. Even the mundane is special. Everything comes with its inherent importance. For example, if we decide to start a family and go easier on our work, that still retains our sense of purpose and being." Bina was unstoppable.

"Pushed the button," Aariz teased her.

"You brought it upon yourself."

"So, you don't think we are insignificant."

"That, we are. Nothing more than specks of dust in the greater scheme of things. But our insignificance shouldn't come in the way of our capacity to exercise agency."

"There's no agency, Bina. We are all just pawns. It's a tiring, exhausting repetition of what happened before. And what happened before is what is happening now. And what is happening now will happen tomorrow as well."

"Humans wouldn't have made any progress had they thought-"

This wasn't going to conclude in any way.

"What became of Sharda, Bina?" Mehar asked the critical thing, trying to be as tactful as she could be; it was Bina's sore point. She had never gotten the chance to delve into the issue with Bina.

"Nothing, Mehar. She is now called Shahida. Lives with that man in Karachi. Contact between her and us had been prohibited. The court decided she was an adult and approved the nikah."

"Oh," Mehar said, shaking her head. But she knew humans

were capable of the most atrocious things and that nothing could be done about that.

"And Kamla *Bua's* family went to India, you told me some time ago?" Aariz pressed further.

"Yes, they went to India. Kamla *Bua* feared that after the court's orders, her other daughter, Rashmi, had somehow become a fitting target, so they went. They stayed in India for six months in Rajasthan, in a camp where other Hindu families from Pakistan were also present. They got ample media attention initially and were hoping something good would come out of it. But as the months passed, they realised they weren't wanted there either. Living became hard, and getting the essentials became a problem. And there was no progress on their citizenship application. So they returned last year."

"Belonging, the eternal human hunt," Aariz spoke softly.

"Funny how a piece of paper can decide so much about a living person. Stamps and ink are probably more worthy than humans." Abhimanyu spoke for the first time.

"Yunhi hamesha ulajhti rahi hai zulm se khalq, na inki rasm nayi hai na apni reet nayi," Mehar quoted Faiz. Everyone stayed silent as a token of agreement.

It has always been our way to resist tyranny. Neither is their oppression new, nor our rebellions.

Aariz had started to lose focus. His head started aching, and these headaches had grown in intensity and frequency over the last couple of weeks. Sometimes, they would be debilitating and imperious to medication. He heard Mehar compliment Bina on her cooking. He was sure the two women would sit together after their husbands had gone to sleep and talk for hours. Aariz asked for everyone's permission to retire to bed.

"Sure, Aariz," Bina said. "Before you go, I hope you know that I find your ideas fascinating. But some things are necessary. Some people need saviours."

"But some people don't need saving, Bina."

Chapter Twenty Seven

EVERY EVENING, a group of folk singers gathers at the Hazuri Bagh between the Badshahi Mosque and the Royal Fort, a little offside the mausoleum of the national poet of the country. While the grand Mughal mosque at one end of the compound teems with prayers five times a day, the *samadhi* of a dead Sikh ruler, along with a Gurdwara, almost hugs the mosque at one side. On the other side, a food street has been set up, where the kothas of dead courtesans have been converted into gorgeous miniatures of eateries. In the lanes behind the street, the fabled Heera Mandi invites travellers to tell them stories about its colourful past, even if it doesn't have many practical gifts to give them anymore, its inventory having dried up in all these years. It's quite some sight there, a holy communion of sin and splendour, piety and debauchery, to be witnessed nowhere but here. People sit in circles around the group of singers as they clear their throats to hit the proper octaves. Some people give them cash, most just swing their heads in all directions with the flow of the music and lyrics. If they don't feel a trance, they pretend they do. Even if they don't understand the classical, intense Punjabi, they act like they do, sometimes letting their heads fall towards their knees as if the words have swatted them from behind. Usually, they sing *Heer* here. They have a collection of the finest of verses from Waris Shah's poetry that they recite with enviable virtuosity. Today, for a change, someone has requested a specific work by Maulana Rumi. The group searches for the lyrics on google, and, placing their phone before them, starts the recital:

"When I die; when my coffin is being taken out,
You must never think I am missing this world.
Don't shed any tears, don't lament or feel sorry. I'm not falling into
a monster's abyss.
When you see my corpse is being carried,
Don't cry for my leaving.
I'm not leaving; I'm arriving at eternal love.
When you leave me in the grave, don't say goodbye.
Remember, a grave is only a curtain for the paradise behind.
You'll only see me descending into a grave; now watch me rise.
How can there be an end? When the sun sets,
Or the moon goes down, it looks like the end,
It seems like a sunset, but in reality, it is dawn.
When the grave locks you up, that is when your soul is freed.
Have you ever seen a seed fall to earth, not rise with a new life?
Why should you doubt the rise of a seed named man?....
When, for the last time, you close your mouth,
Your words and soul will belong to the world of no place, no time."

Chapter Twenty Eight

THE BODY was placed in the centre of their apartment, resting on a charpoy and shrouded in white, coated with roses and Islamic verses. The dead man's expression seemed unfitting for a catastrophe of this sort; it took away from the scene its gravity: the repose on his face almost lending him a semblance of pretence. It was as if a kid was pretending to be asleep, and would burst out giggling as Old Papa would tickle him. And then he would ask Old Papa to tell him a story. And he would take his son into his arms and tell him some quirky story where dead people became alive and started talking, where everything would be and would not be. Mama would scoff at Old Papa for telling a kid such unsuitable stories, but Old Papa would just laugh it off. He knew his boy was brave. And one day, he would leave for the boy to be brave for a very long time.

It seemed he could wake up at any moment, laugh at the people mourning him, and tell them he had duped them. People would start griping, telling him this is not funny and that he needs to lessen his trait of dark humour. He would laugh them off, telling them their hyper-inflated worries made no sense.

Typical Aariz.

But he wouldn't wake up now, Mehar knew.

He wouldn't want to wake up.

Late into the night that day, neighbourhood women kept coming to their apartment long after the body had been buried. Some of Aariz's friends that Mehar knew also came for condolences.

No one from either of their families did.

The women lunged at Mehar and grabbed her, crying hoarse in her ears. They threw themselves around in a vivacious fashion, their wails only pausing momentarily while the food was served; finding the best piece of chicken in the rice was also a part of mourning.

"Look at that poor woman. First divorced, then widowed. At such a young age. How will she spend the rest of her life now? No one will take her. There must be something wrong with her. I have heard her family is into black magic as well. There's some *Bengali Baba* they go to."

Cursed.

"You know me, I am not the one to say this thing or that about someone, but Shareefaan was telling me this girl - *tauba.* Smokes cigarettes and roams around her brother's house like a man. No sense of shame, *bhae.* What can we say, but God has his way of punishing such people."

Evil.

"She has lost her husband - such tragedy - but look at her standing there like nothing has happened, in her freshly ironed clothes, *wah.* Her previous husband also hit her for being a bad character type. She may already be planning to run away with a new lover. For why hasn't she given him any kid in this marriage? You don't know the girls these days."

Slut.

Mehar stood through this all, valiantly, accepting the plethora of unwonted sympathies that came her way without entertaining them. The women resented her for not giving them a show of visitation that they would narrate to others later.

They expected her to dive head-first into a trance, break her bangles, pray to die, and complain to God.

Above all, they wanted to see her scream.

But of course, she wouldn't scream.

* * *

Bina came to Lahore later that night. She had been on duty in the emergency department, where the mobile signals didn't work. When she saw the text on her phone, she left Islamabad straight away. When she reached Aariz and Mehar's apartment, most of the guests had gone. She launched herself at Mehar and cried. Mehar consoled her, and took her to her room, where they sat silent for a while, save for the sobs of Bina, a wedding picture of Aariz and Mehar looking down at them from where it hung above the bed.

"There was no one like Aariz," Bina said after regaining her ability to speak, which wilted soon, "He was such an important person in my life."

"I know." smiled Mehar.

"In all the years I have known him, he's continued to be above what bothers the rest of us. He was just a seed of comfort for those around him, never demanding anything from anyone."

Mehar took a long while to respond.

"Well, he demanded one thing from life. Freedom."

Bina stayed silent.

Up in some world above them that none of them could see, matter became energy and spread in all directions, taking a new form. Not knowing what it was before, not knowing what it would become afterward.

Death.

What ends.

What begins?

"You know Mehar, the Bhagavat Gita says that just as a man discards old clothes and wears new ones, the souls discard old bodies and take on new ones?"

Mehar kept on smiling. She knew Aariz would continue to live; it was a fact that did not reduce itself to validation. Whether in the form of a body, though, she wasn't sure. He may continue to live in the tree that would sprout above his grave, becoming its manure and contributing to its structure, a little bit of Aariz flowing through its xylem and phloem; or maybe get eaten up by the worms that would consume him in his new home, and become a part of them; he'll definitely find some sense of humour there.

He will also continue to live through her.

She looked at the picture of her dead husband hanging above them and sighed, "He was too precious for this world."

"Hmm," Bina agreed, lachrymose.

"Feroze texted me. He is out of the country but says he'll come to visit as soon as he is back."

Mehar changed the topic; she was uncomfortable with grieving, having given up on the practice long ago.

The mention of Feroze did not cause the rising of a tide inside Bina as it otherwise would. She was planning to meet him next month in any case. Maybe her emotional capacities were already consumed by the death of her dear friend.

"You know, Mehar, what Aariz always used to tell me? He used to say that he has never felt for anyone what he felt for you."

Mehar looked at her blankly.

A peal of thunder roared in the air. The gate of the adjoining apartment clanked by its force, opening and closing.

She wanted to scream.

Tears rolled down her eyes, plopping to the floor and becoming steam. More matter became energy.

Bina joined her silently.

Mehar closed her eyes and imagined Aariz: handsome, cheerful, gentle. She imagined his smile exuding a warmth she could never touch, that no one could ever touch. Aariz who was and who was not. Aariz, who had been around her but had always colonized some other dimension of existence. In her imagination, Aariz became a concept.

Was he real?

Bina offered to make tea for both of them. She came back ten minutes later and handed Mehar her cup. In these ten minutes, Mehar had reconciled with the idea of Aariz-the-man and Aariz-the-concept, and had made peace with his death.

Her grief annihilated her.

His relief soothed her.

Grief and relief formed an impassable shield around Mehar, protecting her.

Even in death, Aariz had given her a gift.

After a while, she told Bina.

"He just could not take it anymore."

* * *

On the same day that Aariz died, hordes of people living in ancient valleys in the north-western part of the country bunched around a coffin placed in the open: the women had their hair unbarred, and the men came with ammunition and musical instruments. The solemnity of the setting was dissembled as the drums started beating, the whistles followed, and the men started dancing. This was to continue for three days before the body would be buried. Around forty goats would have to be feasted upon. Every once in a while, someone would start talking about the probities of the dead man, and the music momentarily paused, only to resume when the eulogy had ended. As a new group of people would join the proceedings, shots would be fired into the air.

Qaiser Kalasha, the hotel manager in Chitral who had become Aariz's friend, had died.

All the people gathered were celebrating his death.

For thousands of years, the Kalasha have been celebrating death. Their funerals are carnivals. It started when the God of death, Sajigor, sent a command down from the skies that death shouldn't be mourned; it should be heralded with dance and music. And that is what the Kalasha had been doing for aeons.

* * *

"Papa, what is the age of mourning?" A son asks his father in another world.

"It's infinity, son."

"And the age of celebrating?"

"Infinity."

Chapter Twenty Nine

Bina and Abhimanyu had met by a chance encounter, an encounter that was smoothly engineered by the stars that shine down upon us. The names of those stars were Mehar and Aariz. One of those stars had gone up in the sky; on some days, it appeared even during the day, usually hovering around the sun. It gleamed the brightest.

"But only in the Lion King," Old Papa would laugh.

Abhimanyu worked with an NGO based in the Thar desert. Since shifting to Mirpur Khas, he had been involved in the projects of a Non-Governmental Organisation since its inception, and now was a permanent member of its board. Aariz had met him first in Dubai, and he pitched Mehar the idea of getting Bina settled. Going by Aariz's depiction, Mehar found Abhimanyu agreeable and decent, and recommended Bina to meet him.

Bina agreed, for Aarti's anxious musings if not out of a personal desire. They all met, the four of them, in Lahore. It went better than predicted. Aariz and Mehar chose to retire from the conversation soon after it started, and the ball was thrown toward the potential couple. There was an instant connection between them, if not of the heart, then of the mind.

And it was just as well.

Radha became someone else's wife.

Meera became someone else's wife.

Will someone write such a line about Bina too?

Bina told Abhimanyu about the medical camp she would be interested in arranging in Thar, where malnourished children were dying due to scarce resources. Abhimanyu told her about the water pump installations they had done in the area and the numerous lives impacted by them. His NGO was also documenting the peacocks of Thar and the kinship they had with the people.

"Some Thari women tie *rakhis* to the peacocks. It's riveting to see these dynamics in which human beings can form relationships. Since a brother has to protect a sister who has tied a *rakhi* on him, this practice is the women pledging the life of the peacocks. They have to be alive, because clearly, they cannot protect the women - their sisters - if they are dead. All the while, the women are fleecing the peacocks into a bond that is meant for the safety of not the women, but the peacocks. In this way, the women guarantee the safety of the peacocks, lest a communicable disease breaks out in them and wipes out a part of their population, which has happened before as well."

"Does it work?"

"They believe it does. Their belief makes it work."

After that meeting, Bina and Abhimanyu met three more times - first in Lahore, then Islamabad.

No one really had to propose to the other. They knew the prospect for which they had started meeting, and every agreement of another meeting only cemented their conviction.

There was only one problem.

Abhimanyu was a Dalit, a lower caste, belonging to the Kolhi community of Nagarparkar.

But Bina had decided she would not let this come in the way. She told her father sternly that this was the case, and that it was not up for debate in any way. The conversation lasted for a full two minutes. In a moment of limitless conviction, she also told Shreeshanth he would have to choose between his daughter and society, even when it was unwarranted, as Shree's tacit reservation about Bina's decisions did not deserve such a severe threat. He had given in already. But Bina, for her part, was done with the lines in her life.

The heart wants what it wants.
Sometimes, it wants chaos.

* * *

Feroze opened the door and shook hands with Abhimanyu, smiling at Bina. She reciprocated. He looked sick; Bina could draw his mandibles from atop the skin. He gestured towards them to enter. Bina had been inside the mansion rarely; that too, as a kid. She did not remember any particulars about the place except that it was huge and had many funny statues. She remembered a particularly horrid statue of a woman with snakes skidding over her head and that it lay just inside the main lounge.

It was gone.

Feroze took them straight to the dining room. They sat in chairs that sang songs of another country, and made themselves comfortable. Bina and Abhimanyu sat on one side, and Feroze sat across from them. He started by voicing his grief on the death of Aariz. Bina and Abhimanyu nodded. He couldn't convey the full intensity of his sentiment to them, but he was profoundly jolted by it. When it happened, he was out of the country. He had talked to Mehar the same day, and told her he would come to see her when he was back.

He did not tell anyone that he had come to Lahore straight after returning to the country and went straight to where Aariz lay, now buried under a mound of clay.

That day, a fully grown man cried like an infant in front of another man that lay six feet below him. He embraced the grave, getting mud all over him, and kissed the space where the face of his dearest friend lay underground. He shivered; he asked for forgiveness from Aariz. He spoke aloud all they meant to each other, right from when the two boys became friends in Lahore.

"Aariz, do you remember when we smoked our first cigarette together? Sneaking out of our dorm in the middle of the night, I was so scared that the provost would catch us and report to baba. You proceeded without a hint of care. Oh, how I loved you: fearless and daring. I looked up to you, and you were the only solace in the life of a boy encumbered by ideas of propriety and responsibility. It was only with you that I urged to be free and more like you. And how you would never judge me for anything but would readily understand. You were always the one to give without asking for anything in return. You were my only escape in life. And I had become so dependent on you that I lost my sense of direction when you left for college. I blamed you for showing me the possibility of liberty and leaving me alone in an abyss. Remember Aariz, how we used to share stuff with each other we could never with anyone else? How I could only tell you that it gets so overbearing upholding the legacy of my father and that I wasn't meant for it? That it became tougher for me every day, but I had no way to give up? And you would tell me to take a stand for myself and do as I please. And you would bring in recordings of cricket matches only for me to watch? I still remember the night you told me about what your stepfather did to you. I remember it was raining that night, and we sat on the lawn of one of baba's friends in Zaman Park. That is the only time I have seen you break. You embraced me, hid your head in my pull-over, and sobbed. But I'm so sorry that I had already been irrevocably damaged by then. Instead of understanding your pain, I secretly joyed over having a functioning family unlike yours. And a father who provides for me. I never deserved you. I'm so, so sorry. I would do anything to talk to you only once more, to apologise, to hug you. Can we get that time back? I swear I will do things differently this time! If I was ever myself in my life, it was only when I was with you. Aariz, please come back!"

When Feroze left the graveyard that afternoon, he was shivering with fever. He would never recover from it.

He never went to see Mehar.

Bina shifted in her chair, trying to make herself relaxed.

"Where's Aunty, Feroze?" She asked about his mother as she couldn't be seen around. She had always struck Bina as a kind woman; if only she were in a different place at a different time. Bina did not actually care where she was and was relieved she was spared from exchanging civilities and notes of sympathy with a woman she did not feel anything for. "I am so sorry, aunty, for your loss, even when I feel your husband deserved a lot worse than sudden death, and that he destroyed so much, his son being at the fore of his casualties, but also the ideas of loyalty and friendship. So am I really sorry? No, aunty, let's be honest, I am not. I am not sorry for him, I don't want to admit it, but I am glad he's gone. I am not sorry for you either; you clearly were an abettor. And I am not sorry for not feeling sorry for something I apparently need to be sorry about."

"I sent her to my aunt, her sister, in Germany. Her health had deteriorated here, as everything in this place reminded her of father. We thought a change of place and company might do her good," Bina and Abhimanyu nodded.

Shabbaraat came with the helping staff and started serving already. He recognised Bina but would always only nod at her as if he accepted her existence but never approved of it. Bina did not like Shabbaraat. In her mind, Shabbaraat had always been an extension of Hashmatullah, privy to all his crafty schemes. But a younger Bina didn't know that many in her part of the world waded through life without any options. Options were a luxury for most, next only to air conditioners and chauffeur-driven cars.

Shabbaraat was a witness to the unbreakable friendship between Bina and Feroze. He had seen the kids sneaking together, climbing trees and counting stars. The drivers told him about the kids' adventures together. And all that Shabbaraat knew put him in a perilous position to gauge this relationship. He knew what Hashmat did to Shreeshant, he had been there when the property was transferred, and Bina was denied her due rights. He was sure Feroze would one day fan the same injustice to Bina. Belonging to a family of servants makes you adept at understanding such things; the blood of your masters also starts running through your veins, replacing the iron in your cells with the thoughts of the masters.

Shabbaraat liked Bina. She was a delightful child, brave and adventurous. And Shabbaraat secretly hoped for her to end her friendship with Feroze, as this only translated to doom. He could never say this; of course, this wasn't his place to do so. But giving Bina a cold stare every so often, he hoped she would understand.

In his mind, he was constantly being Bina's saviour.

He didn't know that Bina was the saviour for others; she didn't need any saviours for herself.

But did she need saving?

"There you go," said Feroze. "There's rice, there's *pallo* machi, there's…"

Bina started serving Abhimanyu. Feroze eyed her flatly.

They ate in silence, except for the occasional remarks of Feroze like "I am very happy for you," "You guys look great together," and the like. Bina answered these with equally half-meaning remarks from her side, "Feroze, you should get married now," "I will find you a good Sindhi girl," "You will definitely win the elections next time," and the like.

By the time they had finished the dinner, they had run out of any more mundane comments to make. They shifted to the lounge, where green tea was to be served. After it was, Feroze told all his staff to go away.

Bina had not expected this to be as awkward as it was. No one was really talking. Abhimanyu, anyway, wasn't the one to talk a lot; he always said silence was a survival skill for desert dwellers. Feroze and Bina were also out of words.

Because what was there to say?

The silence of the room was amplified by the vehemence of the seconds' hand of the large grandfather clock that stood in the corner of the room.

Tick, tick, tick...

So Bina made a flogging effort.

"We are going abroad for our honeymoon, Feroze. To Europe. Only God knows how much savings we had to chip in to make this possible. And it's the first time I am going outside of Pakistan. Abhimanyu has been to Dubai, I think…." She looked at Abhimanyu, who nodded inattentively.

Feroze wasn't listening. He was looking at something in the distance without a focus in his eyes.

Bina sat confused for a moment, and then went on to tell him something only Mehar knew.

"Feroze, I have some good news. We are expecting!"

The lens in Feroze's eyes contracted to converge his sight on the woman that sat before him. Something tanked inside Feroze's head. First, he thought the inherited silence was back but realised it wasn't. Some shocks - and reactions - don't owe themselves to the legacies.

"Well, congratulations!" Feroze tried to smile.

Bina adjusted in her seat. Abhimanyu rubbed his hand on hers. They smiled at Feroze.

And then it happened.

The unforgivable. The unforgettable.

The seven stages of grief forgot what stage they were in and gathered to occupy and vanquish the man, undoing his being and waging war on all that remained of his capacities.

Feroze stood up and started shouting at the top of his voice, which gave in owing to the surge of emotions in his voice.

"Why did you do this to me, Bina? All my life, I have never been myself. I have never done much of my own volition. But if there was anything I wanted for myself, it was you. I have lost Aariz. I have asked for your pardon. I have tried to undo what I have done. But why do you hurt me like this? Tell me, what should I do? What was my fault? What could be a child's fault? I did not kidnap that girl.

I did not commit fraud with your father. What do I do now? And today, you have come to announce that you have slept with another man and are now carrying his baby? Are you heartless or insane?"

Bina's heart stopped beating. There was a lot to counter this with. She had a lot to say.

But she didn't.

She will not allow herself to be sucked back into the black hole she came from.

"We'll take your leave now, Feroze!"

"Of course, you will." The fever had become a fire, it was all set to scorch everything, and this time no divine injunction was to come from the skies to douse it.

What happened next is a jittery succession of events, and it's hard to say what happened when.

Feroze pulled out a metallic object from his pocket; Abhimanyu dived in front of Bina; the guards entered as Feroze called them and pulled Bina away, someone screamed from afar, and then there was the sound of a gunshot.

It lasted only a while.

Or it could have been a century.

Chapter Thirty

A WOMAN admits a man to her place of belonging, taking him inside the Delhi Gate. The sun burnishes her hair, giving them a brownish sheen before recasting them into a transparent hue. The earrings in her ears radiate, swinging across the air in a pendulous motion. He is charmed by them, the light entering the sapphires at the base of the earrings, ejecting into a glare that makes little rainbows transcending all directions. He is in awe of her beauty, of her other world-ness. He is a bit cagey at first, not being used to the environment of the establishment.

"Come, I'll lead the way."

She extends her hand forward.

He takes it.

Holds it firmly, promising never to let it go.

The woman laughs.

The stars twinkle. In her eyes. And the sky.

They move in quick succession across the lanes, careful not to bump into anything. The woman is telling the man a lot of anecdotes. Everything has an association with her. A while ago, she was chattering about how good the mango pickles of that shop are, then she exclaimed that this market was established during the reign of Akbar the Great, now she is on to tell him about some *haveli* that has ghosts.

He is not listening.

He is only looking at her, smiling like a fool.

The woman takes the man along through the journey of a thousand years; spellbound, he is enthused by her comfort with the process. It is as if she were a Mughal princess taking him through her Fort.

No one notices them. They keep on accelerating through the lanes; there's a monument at every turn, they laugh.

Then they start flying.

They glide past the multi-colored clothes that houses have on full display on the lines. They pass through the antiquated radio sets playing old songs they both know by heart. They fly past the shimmering lights of countless colours set up for Eid Milad.

They go up in the air and land on a rooftop. Everything is beautiful from this angle. He grabs her by the arms.

They look at each other.

Their eyesights converge on a point midway between them, becoming a tiny diamond.

It bolts into the air, and transforms into a lone cloud.

It starts raining.

The man advances toward the woman, both drenched.

They become so close that raindrops cannot find a way to escape.

Their skins touch. They smile. The embrace is hardened.

They taste each other.

Water.

Sweat.

Salt.

And… blood.

Mehar wakes up with a start; she remembers she has to meet Bina the next day.

Chapter Thirty One

TWO WHITE silhouettes dart across the river Indus. At their side is a child, but it is hard to notice at a cursory glance. On drawing closer, it is revealed that a single sheet of white cloth covers all three people.

A man, a woman, and a child.

They enter the water, but it doesn't take them. They walk over it, unmoved by its waves.

After crossing the water, they emerge onto a silent field streaked by date trees.

The child opens his mouth, and a date drops into it.

He chokes, then swallows it, and laughs. The parents also laugh.

The woman grouses about her clinic, and the man grins at her.

The man says something about a political alliance, and the woman smiles at him.

They both feel incredulously fortunate to be in each other's company.

In the distance, someone is milking their cows. A little while off, a group of women attired exuberantly sing *"Khair Neem Kay Neechay"* and circle around, their heads covered, white bangles ending at their elbows. They start jigging in circles, their arms falling by their sides as they advance towards each other. Someone starts playing the flute in the distance.

Is it Krishna?

But it could be Ranjha as well.

As they go forth, silently, without having the need for any words, they encounter a lake. The man takes the baby and jumps across.

The woman cannot jump.

She sees a pitcher lying on the bank of the lake and uses it.

She clasps it, immersing it in the water, and floats towards the other side, thrusting water in the opposite direction.

The baby jumps and claps. The man looks at her, confident she will come to them.

She is afraid for a split second she might drown, the pitcher would give away, but then she concedes nothing can come between them anymore. Blind dolphins come to her aid, they propel the pitcher forward. She knows the water of Mother Indus has immortalised her, freed them of all the twines that had pulled them apart.

She reaches across.

She holds the man and the baby close to her heart.

It beats assertively, emitting ardour.

The sun comes down to borrow some of her heart's warmth. It promises it will return it.

They agree.

They don't let go of each other.

The sun goes up in the sky and smiles down upon them, telling them it will rise again tomorrow, only to see them.

They smile.

The baby claps harder.

They sleep beneath a date tree, their pulsating bodies whisked together.

But when they wake up, everything has turned dark forever. They realise the sun has broken its promise.

Bina wakes up with a start; she remembers she has to meet Mehar the next day.

Epilogue

AN OLD Qingchi rickshaw halts to a stop in a place steaming with bustle. An old woman gets out of it, her hair dishevelled and her expression frenetic, and she testily hands over to the rickshaw driver only half of the amount decided.

"You almost took my life away! Driving like a sisterfucking maniac!" she shouts.

The driver curses her back, howling at her to return, but she has already faded into the buzzing crowd; it is difficult to locate her anymore. She courses through the lanes, screaming at motorcycle drivers to screw themselves and get out of her sight. After turning into a broader street, she buys flowers for forty rupees, and then takes another handful for free because she finds the flowers stale. ("Death to your mother, thief!") The seller doesn't retaliate, he is used to the tantrums of the hag. She is anyway going to die soon, he consoles himself.

The woman passes a police checkpoint ("Touch me like you touch your mother, scum," she tells the police personnel - who simply takes a side) and enters an enthralling complex. A fire burns in front of the main shrine. She curses herself for forgetting to buy candles, and asks some other people to give her some, but after facing a tirade of refusals, ("May you burn where water cannot reach you!") throws some of the flowers into the fire. The place has a lot more people than usual, as the Mela Chiraghaan - the festival of lights - is going on with full fanfare. It would continue for the next three days.

On the other side of the fire, two women meet. It has been quite some time since the four of them had met at the same spot, and now only two pilgrims remained - seeing each other after six months.

The women hug each other, with longing and despair.

The hag passes them by and sees some tears rolling down their cheeks.

She had also cried once.

It doesn't help.

One of the two women carries a baby; she looks at it fondly, kisses it, and then hands it over to the other woman. The other woman takes it eagerly, without any question, and starts cradling it in her arms. There was probably some understanding between them already.

The two women take a quiet spot and sit in silence for some time, neither in a hurry to expedite the meeting.

The tears had stopped.

Now was the time for secrets.

But what was there to say?

The hag opens her arms before the fire and starts churning out verses from Shah Hussain's poetry, in a voice that is as discordant as it is jarring.

"Oh mother, oh mother, how do I tell...

The pain of separation!"

"I am taking over his consultancy firm."

"I am going to England tomorrow."

For a moment, the women feel they have been joined by the two other pilgrims; a puff of breeze mistakes them into the hunch. But they know it was impossible.

Some pilgrimages had been completed.

"Abhimanyu's body was found in a field off Sukkur."

"Aariz had paid Ahmad to divorce me."

There was silence.

But what was there to say?

They knew.

They embrace each other again, and smile at the gifts each had given to the other.

They take a long time before they let go. They aren't sure if they will ever meet again. Some pilgrimages take you to wayward paths that consume you; they abandon you through deserts, mountains, and rivers, and steeling yourself for the perpetual odyssey remains the only available option; looking back only impedes the sacred journey you're already upon.

The baby cowers and moans in the arms of its new mother. She takes it to her breast.

The old woman is incorrigible.

"Driven mad with spikes,

The pain of separation fills my thoughts."

Around them, there's a fuss; people huddle together in the sitting area where langar was soon to start. Adolescent boys buy cheap, potent hashish from the dealers, smuggled all the way from Waziristan, their virgin escapade into the world of drugs. A group of people starts dancing lunatically at the other end of the complex. Some people kneel before the grave of the saint; some give them disapproving looks. A woman carrying a DSLR with a telescopic lens is being escorted by her security guards, and the whirling dervishes are striking different poses for her. With every gust of air that makes its way towards the fire, some of the many lit *diyas* give away their fire, only to be re-kindled by someone else, continuing the cycle of hope.

And some things are left unsaid. The air is sober with their load; they could have grazed the words if only they had spread out their hands to touch them. But they don't need to. Sometimes, hiding is the best way of sharing. But this hiding doesn't come from a place of suspicion - it buds from an unfailing, undeterred trust.

But what was there to say?

They knew.

They understood.

One woman does not tell the other that the morning her husband's body was found in the fields, Shabbaraat had told her there was found another body as well.

One woman does not tell the other that the night before her

husband died, Zainab had seen this woman sneak a little bottle marked "poison" into her room.

"Wander looking for Ranjha Ranjha...

But Ranjha is with me."

It is still an hour before the two women depart, over and on to their pilgrimages.

Some pilgrimages had not yet been completed.

But one gate had opened.

One line had blurred.

Glossary

Nikah: The marriage contract in Islamic Law.

Samadhi: A special building made to hold the dead body of an important person or to remind people of that person. Also refers to the highest state of mental concentration that unites people with the ultimate reality.

Vanvas: Literal: Residing in a forest. An exile, sometimes taken voluntarily but mostly forced. Features as a harsh penalty in Hindu epics of Ramayan and Mahabharat.

Urs: The death anniversary of a Sufi saint, often celebrated with much enthusiasm and show.

Kotha: Brothel.

Rakhi: A bracelet or amulet made of thread that sisters tie around their brothers' wrist, traditionally in Hindu culture.

Haveli: A traditional mansion, typically associated with wealthy families.

Diya: A cup shaped oil lamp made of clay.

Ayat Ul Kursi: The Throne Verse, regarded as one of the greatest verses from the Holy Quran.

Salam: A common greeting in Muslim culture.

Glossary

Khaala: Maternal aunt. Often used as a term of endearment for elder women.

Yaar: A friendly form of addressing someone.

Azaan: The Muslim call to prayer.

Chehlum: Forty days, the traditional length of mourning in Islamic tradition.

Gora: A while person, sometimes used derogatorily.

Bua: Title of respect used for older women.

Baaradari: A pavilion with twelve doors.

Sahab: A polite title for a man.

Sardaar: Title of nobility.

Author Bio

Muhammad Asif Nawaz was born and raised in Abbottabad. He studied to be a doctor, getting registered with the General Medical Council in United Kingdom, before joining the Pakistan Administrative Service. He has served at various stations in Punjab, Balochistan and Gilgit Baltistan. Asif entertains a penchant for travelling and history, as evident in this book as well. He also grapples with filmmaking and photography at times, and one of the photographs he clicked of Takht e Bahi now hangs in the permanent gallery of the Museum of Asian Art in Humboldt Forum, Berlin. He has been published in various national and international magazines, but at 33 years of age, "The Pilgrims" is his first novel. He can be reached on Twitter and Instagram @asifnz.